LET LOVE WIN

A.D. ELLIS

ONE

SKYLER BYRD

RAIN RAN in rivulets down my face as I knocked on the door. As much as I despised the rain, I hated crying even more, so I welcomed the wetness and hoped it would disguise my tears.

No way was it going to hide my black eye. I'd left way too quickly to grab my makeup, so I was going to have to make-do with the *very* few supplies I had in my backpack for a cover-up. At least until I could get to the store. And, fuck it. I was going back to get my clothes and belongings. No matter what.

I knocked again and prayed that this was the right house. I'd been determined to *never* see my parents or my brother again—not after the way they'd treated Trent when I'd come out to them—but three years of verbal and emotional abuse at the hands of my so-called boyfriend had finally culminated in a punch to my face. I'd been forced to swallow my anger, hurt, and pride and turn to my older brother, Charlie.

I shivered in the rain and worried once again that maybe I'd recalled the address wrong. I was pretty sure Charlie had been living here for at least a few years or more, but the longer I stood there, the more concerned I became. I'd only driven by a couple times—partly out of curiosity and partly to fuel my anger on days when I was missing my family more than normal.

Maybe Charlie had peeked out and seen me and decided to ignore me. Honestly, after the way I went off on him and my parents, I probably wouldn't blame him. I wasn't ready to admit they'd been *right* about Trent—I definitely wasn't ready to say I'd been *wrong*—but not for the first time, I wondered if I'd ruined any and all chances of reconciliation with my family. Three years ago, that wouldn't have bothered me. Lately, though? It was a definite worry.

With one last pounding on the door, I waited a full thirty seconds—then another thirty just in case—before turning to leave. Beyond the roar of thunder and rain, I heard a voice behind the door just as I turned.

"Pause it, the pizza's here," the voice called out.

The door swung open.

The man frowned. "You're not the pizza guy."

My stomach dropped to my knees just as my heart soared to my throat. Donovan Badger. *Van* as I'd known him growing up. My very first crush—on the straight guy no less. The fodder to my endless nights of jacking off. My first heartache when Charlie went off to college and Van left to travel abroad.

Van.

The tall, broad, scruffy-looking gentle giant.

Van.

The very last person I'd expected to see on the other side of that door.

Van.

My brother's best friend.

"Van?" I croaked.

He scowled and studied me before his eyes went comically wide. "Holy shit! Skyler?"

I nodded as hot tears mixed with cold rain on my face.

Van reached for me and every single bit of grit and determination I'd gathered to hold myself together since the moment I left the house I shared with Trent fell away and I crumbled into Van's arms.

"Charlie!" Van hollered over his shoulder. "Get in here!"

As I snuggled into Van's chest—feeling horrible that I was soaking him to the skin—I heard footsteps and then my brother's voice.

"What the…" Charlie started and quickly pulled me from Van's strong embrace. "Sky, what happened?" He held my quivering chin in his hand and studied my face. With a scowl and a curse, he dropped his hand and hugged me close. "Shit, Sky. I never thought I'd see you again." He shifted and led me to the kitchen table where he pressed me gently into a chair.

"I'm going to get some towels and clothes," a woman said from somewhere in the room.

"Skyler, are you hungry? Food? Coffee? What do you want?" Van asked. Always the caretaker. He'd *always* been the one to make sure I was safe and fed and looked after when we were younger.

I trembled. The cold, the fear, the sadness, the uncertainty had all jumbled together and become too much. As a senior in college, I was in my student teaching semester and I had class on Monday. I couldn't miss it. I was required to teach all day, every day at this point and I'd be damned if fucking Trent was going to mess it up for me. Besides, those Kindergarten babies brought me life so I wouldn't miss it for the world.

But for the moment, I was man enough to admit that I was overwhelmed and needed help. I'd get through the weekend and figure something out. Until then?

"Tea?" I asked, surprised at how shaky and raspy my voice was. "And whatever food you have. Crackers or something easy. I don't expect you to feed me a full meal."

Van smiled softly and ruffled my dripping hair like he used to do when I was a child. *You were always just a kid to Van*, I thought. "You're in luck. We've got a shit ton of pizza on the way. I'll make some tea to warm you up until then."

"You're staying here tonight," Charlie stated and frowned when I started to protest. "Do you have somewhere else to go?" he challenged.

I shook my head and dropped my chin to my chest. I was basically homeless. The house was in Trent's name—something he reminded me of often.

"Just as well because I have no plans on getting my baby brother dry and warm and then letting him go traipsing off into the night after not seeing him for three years." Charlie glanced toward Van. "Hey, hold on the tea." He turned to me. "How about a shower, warm clothes, and then you can warm up and get some food. Sound okay?"

The dramatic, immature part of me that had always flared up when I felt like I needed to prove myself to my family tried to roar to life. But I was exhausted and cold and I didn't have the energy to argue. So, I just nodded.

The woman returned with a towel. "I put some of Charlie's clothes in the bathroom for you—Van's would be way too big. There are towels in the closet. Feel free to use any of the soap or shampoo." She gently placed the towel on my lap.

I quickly used it to soak up the wetness from my hair and face. "Thank you. I'm sorry I'm getting your floor all wet."

Charlie waved away my concern. "It'll dry. Sky, this is my fiancé, Kendall. She's a nurse. Kendall, this is my brother."

"Hi, Skyler. Nice to meet you. I've heard a lot of stories about you," the broad-shouldered, brown-haired, pretty woman smiled kindly as she stood next to Charlie. They made a great-looking couple.

I winced as I wondered at all the stories I was sure my brother had told Kendall.

"They weren't *that* bad," Charlie teased with a chuckle as he pointed toward a hallway. "Go take a shower. Then we'll eat and talk."

Like a zombie, I shuffled past the three curious and concerned faces and made my way through a very nice house to a clean and organized bathroom decorated in a red and blue lighthouse theme. Locking the door behind me, I leaned on the sink and gasped at my appearance. My dark, floppy-on-top brown hair was a mess of wetness plastered to my forehead. My usual stylish stubble made me look like a tired old man rather than a trendy twenty-four-year-old. My dark eyes—usually sparkly and laughing—stared back at me dully. My skin was pale with the only splash of color being the red and purple swollen skin around my left eye where Trent had left his mark.

I shivered. The cold of the rain and emotional drain of the day were getting to me. *Emotional drain of the day*? Okay, so Trent had been emotionally draining me for over three years.

We'd met during our first year of college. I'd known I was gay since a very young age. Okay, maybe that wasn't accurate. I'd known I was stubborn as hell, more dramatic than a movie star, and *different* since a very young age. It wasn't until the summer I was ten that I realized I liked guys. That was the summer I fell in major puppy-love with Charlie's best friend, Van. I crushed on him for six long years—and learned all about unreciprocated love—and I was devastated when Charlie left for college and Van went off to travel trails around the world.

Looking back, I probably could have told my family I was gay long before I did. But that dramatic, stubborn streak was strong and I, for some reason, convinced myself it wasn't the time.

When I got to college, I slept with pretty much any guy who had a heartbeat. Okay, again, maybe not accurate. I slept around. A lot. But I was pretty picky. The guys had to be cute and kind at least. Toward the end of my first year, I met Trent at a party. Linebacker build, sweet smile, piled compliments on me, and wanted to fuck me like nobody's business. I loved that he gave me attention and seemed to want to show me off. We went on a few dates, had sex more than a few times, and talked about what the next year would look like for us.

Trent wanted to move off campus, but he needed someone to split rent with him. My room and board were paid for, but living off-campus sounded so mature and responsible. We made plans to live together and sort of fell into being boyfriends as our freshman year wound down.

The day my parents and Charlie came to help me pack and move home for the summer, I made a speech about how I was gay, Trent was my boyfriend, and if they didn't like it they'd never see me again.

Dramatic, remember?

In hindsight, the whole thing would have maybe gone over better if we weren't all sweating our asses off, starving, and lifting heavy objects. Oh, and maybe if Trent hadn't been yelling at me, belittling me, and rude to my family.

But did my immature ass see any of that?

Hell no.

All I saw was that my parents and Charlie didn't like Trent. As in they didn't like him from the moment they met him. Even before I announced he was my boyfriend. I got defensive. I got stubborn. I got angry. When my parents and brother tried to speak to me privately to let me know moving off campus to live with Trent wasn't the best idea—and that they all thought Trent was being a complete asshole toward me—I defiantly shook them off, accused them of not accepting me because of my sexuality, and stormed off with Trent.

For a few weeks, living on my own with my boyfriend was pure bliss. Sex whenever and wherever—Trent was *very* happy to have found *the perfect little bottom* who loved to suck his dick. Honestly, that should have been one of the first bad signs. No, the *first* bad sign should have been the way he treated me and acted around my family. But tiffs and arguments would end with Trent apologizing and swearing he'd do better. And I believed him every time—even though a part of me was very well-aware that he *never* changed.

Anyway, we both got jobs to save up for rent. We were taking classes during the school year so our work hours would get cut. I broached the subject of my senior year with Trent and explained that I wouldn't be able to work much, if at all, during my student teaching semester.

He'd laughed and said I'd be lucky if he kept my ass around for that long. Then he'd apologized, said he was *just joking*, and assured me that we'd have plenty of money saved up by then and I could take the semester off of working while he covered the rent.

Over the next few years, I missed my parents and Charlie, but I was stupidly determined to make them pay. As time went by, I was able to convince myself that my parents and Charlie didn't like the fact I was gay and they simply used Trent as their out. Trent kept the story I told myself fueled and constantly reminded me of how they didn't accept me. He also made sure I knew *he* was the one who took me in. *He* was the one who owned the house—his name was on the lease, not mine. *He* was the one who deserved my love and attention.

I began to regret moving off campus about midway through my sophomore year. Trent made fun of me constantly—always *just joking* and I was just being *too sensitive*. He was a lazy bum who couldn't keep a job, wasted his money on shit purchases, and expected me to keep the house clean. The only thing he did as far as house chores was to cook. He considered himself an amazing cook and would make these huge meals—which we often couldn't afford—and then leave a kitchen full of dishes for me to clean up.

But what was I going to do? I'd forfeited my room and board by moving off campus. I'd screwed over everything with my family—and I wasn't yet desperate enough to go crawling back with my tail between my legs—I refused to become one of those kids who leaves but has to go back home and then gets stuck there forever. Plus, I was convinced they hated me because I was gay. I was stuck with Trent and the whole situation until I graduated and could get a job. I hoped and prayed that I'd be able to land a teaching job quickly once I was out of school. Or maybe Trent really would change.

And then all of Trent's rage and self-centeredness and anger came to a head during yet another argument. Sex and money were the topics as usual. Not enough of either, and he continued to misspend our money along with using sex to control me. We'd been yelling at each other while I washed yet another pile of dirty dishes after King of the House had made steaks that were only so-so. I'd noticed his cutting board was warped, so I'd tried to fix it and ended up breaking it.

You'd have thought I'd broken a favorite toy the way Trent came at me. He called me terrible names and shoved me. When I cried out and yelled back for him to calm down, I'd replace it, Trent balled up his fist and socked me in the eye.

All of my regrets and fears and misgivings over the situation I'd found myself in came roaring through my head. I'd grabbed my backpack, wallet, and phone and left. Luckily,

I hadn't let Trent convince me that we really only needed his vehicle, and I had a car. After driving around for nearly three hours, I'd finally admitted that Charlie was my best bet. I no longer had his number because Trent had bought the two of us matching phones on a new plan—I think he just wanted to be able to control who I was calling and communicating with; he constantly reminded me that he could track everything I did on that phone.

With a gasp, I turned from the mirror and yanked my phone from the wet pocket of my jeans. I wasn't sure if Trent was worried about me or just angry, but his fifty-some texts weren't something I could deal with at that moment. I powered-down the phone and tossed it on the counter. I hated the fact that he likely knew where I was. I hoped he wouldn't cause a problem.

Shaking away the bad memories—although, I actually felt guilty when I let myself feel like a victim; I didn't have it nearly as bad as a lot of others was what I always told myself —I stripped from my wet clothes and turned on the shower.

I lost track of time as I let the warm water wash over me. Once I was warm and clean, I climbed from the shower. As I dried off, I wondered about the living situation between Charlie, Kendall, and Van. Did Van live here? Was he just visiting? Kendall indicated she didn't give me Van's clothes because they'd be too big, so apparently, he lived with them.

Once I was dressed, I gathered my wet clothes and exited the bathroom. I found the whole little gang sitting in the living room eating pizza. "Hey, can I wash these?" I asked, feeling embarrassed, out of place, and humbled.

"Yep, the washer is ready. Just go throw them in and shut the lid." Charlie gestured toward the little laundry room.

When I returned, my stomach growled and my face heated.

"Sit down and eat," Van ordered. "There's soda for now. I'll fix you tea later."

We ate in silence for a few moments, but I knew questions were coming.

"You ready to talk?" Charlie asked.

"Hey, he looks like he's about to fall over. Let's give him the night, let him rest, and we can all talk in the morning," Van stated as if there was to be no argument. He'd always been a kind of buffer between me and my somewhat steamroller brother.

Charlie glared at his best friend, but softened when Kendall placed a hand on his leg. "Yeah, okay." He glanced my way. "We've got a little spare room—kinda more like an office right now—but it's got a futon in it. You can sleep there."

I nodded and swallowed a bite of pizza. "Thank you."

Charlie's eyes bore into mine. "I mean it. The room is yours. Whatever happened, whatever you need, you're welcome here indefinitely."

I shot a look around at all three of them and saw nothing but smiles and nods. My eyes burned and I gritted my teeth against the tears. "Thank you," I whispered.

When I'd eaten my fill, I passed on the tea and attempted to keep my eyes open.

"Let's get some ice for that eye," Kendall said and pulled me from the couch. "Van, can you get the office ready? There are blankets in the hall closet."

A few minutes later, I'd brushed my teeth with a new toothbrush and had an ice pack on my painful eye. Kendall begged off to go to bed because of an early shift. Charlie explained he was running down to Byrd and Badger to check on things—which hit me like a ton of bricks; had I been so self-centered and consumed in all things Trent for so long that I'd not even realized the two-year-old brewery in town that boasted ours and Van's last name was owned by them? Definitely a lot of talking to do the next day.

"Didn't know if you had a charger, so I put one on the desk. The pillow is an extra," Van gestured toward the futon. "You can leave it like that or pull it out; it's pretty comfortable."

I tossed my backpack to the floor, set my phone, wallet, and keys on the desk, and smiled gratefully. "Thank you. This is perfect. I'm really sorry to have come in and caused chaos like this."

Van scowled. "Are you kidding? Charlie's been waiting for the day you finally came home. This may not be *home* home, but he purposely bought this house with the idea that we could have extra room in case you ever needed us. We'll turn this into a bedroom in no time flat."

My sleepy head couldn't process what he was saying and a tear ran down my face. Had I wasted so much of my life on Trent when my brother and Van had been *right here* waiting for me?

Van chucked my chin and wrapped a large arm around my shoulders. "We'll catch up tomorrow. But never doubt that you've been missed and you're wanted here."

I let Van hold me for a split-second longer than what was probably appropriate for a friend hug and nodded my head against his chest. His warm, protective embrace was a salve to my brokenness.

That night, I slept alone for the first time in over three years, but I felt freer than I had in ages.

TWO

DONOVAN "VAN" BADGER

I CLEANED up the pizza boxes and sodas in a daze as I thought about how quickly we'd gone from playing a video game to Skyler showing up on the doorstep. Checking the time, I knew Charlie would be at Byrd and Badger for a while still, so I grabbed my phone and keys and headed down to offer a hand.

The downpour Skyler had gotten caught in had tapered off to just a light rain. I parked behind Byrd and Badger Brews and let myself in through the back door.

Charlie had gone to college for a business degree while I'd taken off to explore the world and find myself. We'd kept in touch and when I came back to the states, I had no doubts about moving to the busy little college town up the road from where we'd grown up. As long as my best friend was there, I planned to be there.

Charlie and I had been thick as thieves from the time we met as toddlers. My grandmother raised me and she was a neighbor of the Byrd family. Charlie and I—and later Skyler— grew up together and spent hundreds, maybe even thousands, of hours playing in the backyard. Even when we were teens, the backyard and basement were the perfect hangouts. We had other friends, but *Charlie and Van* were a constant. When my grandmother passed away my senior year, I'd packed up all of my questions and curiosities, my fears and longings, and my desire for something *more* and headed off to the other side of the world.

I'd missed home and Charlie every damn day. Hell, I'd even missed Skyler. He was such a spaz, so stubborn, so fucking dramatic about *everything*, but I'd missed him all the same. But traveling and being on my own allowed me to discover the real me and I'd come home refreshed and ready to take on the world.

With my best friend by my side.

Charlie and I had spent months brainstorming ideas for our business. Charlie had the degree, I had the world experience, and we were determined to make whatever business we started a huge success.

One day while hashing out ideas at a kinda crummy brewery outside of our hometown, I'd grimaced at the flavor of the house beer as I'd glanced around the establishment. "Fuck," I'd growled, "we could do so much better than this." I'd waved my hand at the place.

Charlie had started to speak. Closed his mouth. Gaped like a damn fish a couple times. Then smiled like he'd just won the lottery. "You are *so* right. We *could* do so much better than this." He'd raised a brow and waited for me to catch on.

"A brewery?" I'd asked. "Fuck, that's so perfect. Brew some of our own beer and cider, offer local beers and ciders and liquor, have some kick ass food, great environment. Local talent on certain nights. *Fuck*. How did it take so long for us to come to this?"

And at that moment, in a sticky booth in a dark corner of a now-defunct brewery, Charlie Byrd and Donovan Badger penned the first draft of a business plan for Byrd and Badger Brews.

The brewery had been a huge success—so much so that we were thinking of possibly expanding to a couple other college towns—and there was nothing better than working alongside my best friend every day.

I stepped into the office where I found Charlie busy with paperwork. He glanced up and smiled tiredly.

"Today took a turn, huh?" I asked as I grabbed two ciders from the tiny fridge and tossed one to him.

Charlie popped the top and rolled his eyes. "Understatement."

"How you feeling?" I knew Charlie had never given up hope that Sky would eventually come around.

He took a deep breath. "Relieved? Scared? Hopeful? All three? Plus, about ten more." Charlie swigged his cider. "It's so weird to spend so long imagining the day your brother might show up and then, *boom* right in the middle of a video game, he's at your door."

"What do you think happened?" I took a sip from my can and savored the flavor. We really did make fucking great cider. And beer. And our food was damn good.

Charlie frowned. "You saw his eye. I'm assuming that fucker he called a boyfriend hit him. First time? I don't know. But even if Trent hasn't been physically abusive up until now, I know without a doubt he's an asshole who doesn't treat Sky the way he deserves to be treated." He ran a hand over his face. "I *really* want to hope that this was the last straw and Sky will be as determined now to stay away from Trent as he was back then to stay away from us." Charlie massaged his temple. "He needs to be away from Trent. Skyler is amazing and I want him safe. I want him with us. You're still okay with him living with us?"

I nodded. "That's always been the plan, right?" I took

another drink and smiled. "Damn little spaz Skyler grew up to be quite the looker." I hadn't seen Sky since I left when he was sixteen.

Charlie's eyes darted to mine and then he scowled. "Don't. That's not even funny. He's completely off limits. I know where your dick has been and it's not to come anywhere close to my baby brother. You got me?"

I raised my hands in surrender—although a tiny part of me sighed with disappointment that Charlie was immediately *so* against me and Skyler. "Relax. I'm sure he doesn't think of me as anything but his brother's best friend."

Charlie rolled his eyes. "Are you forgetting the six-year crush that kid had on you?"

"Damn shame I took so long to figure out I like guys. That could have been fun." Then I winced. "Never mind. I just thought of the ages and realized that sounded creepy as fuck."

We both laughed.

I'd finally come to terms with a lot of things in my life as I trekked across the world. One of those things was my sexuality. I had no parents around to come out to. My grandmother would have loved me no matter what. So, Charlie was the only person I had to worry about.

I'd called him and told him about a week after I'd figured it out. Honestly, if he'd shut me out or ended our friendship, I would have been shocked—and devastated, of course. Charlie had always thought Skyler was gay; he was always saying he wished Sky trusted the family enough to just come out. But Charlie also understood that it was a personal thing and couldn't happen on anyone else's timeline. But Charlie had been one of the most supportive brothers to a gay-but-not-out sibling I'd ever seen. So, I really hadn't expected him to be different with me.

Charlie had taken to me being gay as easily as a fish to

water. Nothing had changed between us other than he now pointed out guys I might think were hot instead of girls.

"Does Skyler know I'm gay?" I asked before taking the last sip of cider.

"No!" Charlie exclaimed with a bit too much force. "And I don't think you need to tell him."

It was my turn to scowl. "Charlie, he's going to be living with us and you want me to not tell him I'm gay?"

"Would you tell him if you were straight?" Charlie pressed and I rolled my eyes.

"Unfortunately, *straight* is the default that everyone seems to assume. Most people don't have to announce they're straight. So, I'm supposed to just hide who I am? Do you want me to not date? Pretend to be straight?" I raised a brow. I had no doubt Charlie would recognize the stupidity of what he was saying if I waited long enough.

Charlie huffed. "Fuck, I don't know. No. No, I'd never ask you to do that. It's just, come on, Van. He's my baby brother. You're my best friend. It's got disaster written all over it."

"Charlie, my dear hetero, you're assuming that just because Sky and I are both gay that we'll automatically be attracted to each other and bone on every surface of the house."

"Dear God," Charlie winced, "please do not *ever* talk about boning my brother again."

I waggled my brows. "Maybe I want *him* boning me. I'm vers you know. I like to bone and *be* boned." I pretended to consider the situation. "Do you think Sky only bottoms? Strictly a top? Nah, I'm thinking he's vers too."

Charlie narrowed his eyes. "Stop. Just stop. Look, I don't mean to be rude, but you can't argue that you've slept around *a lot* since you figured things out. I don't want Sky hurt."

"Oh, so I'd automatically be the one hurting him?" I pursed my lips. "What if he broke my heart?"

"See? Right there. How would I deal with a brokenhearted brother *or* best friend? Don't put me in the middle. There are plenty of guys out there for you *and* for Sky. You guys don't need each other." Charlie's eyes begged me to agree.

"What if he's my soulmate? The one to open my slutty heart and show me what true love really means?" I teased. Honestly, I hadn't thought about Sky as anything but a kid for years. Seeing him on the front porch had been a stark reminder that Skyler Byrd was all grown up. And fucking hot as hell. Part of me wanted to tell Charlie to fuck off; part of me wanted to respect his wishes and keep Skyler as just a friend.

Charlie's face paled and he took a deep breath. "I just don't want to be in the middle, see either of you hurt, have to clean up a mess on either side. Can't you just fuck other guys and leave Sky alone?"

I chuckled. "How about this? Sky and I are friends. I won't purposely try to get him in my bed for a one-n-done—truly, that would be awkward as fuck if he's living with us—and I'll only pursue something with him if *he* indicates it's something he wants? Does that work?"

Charlie narrowed his eyes.

"Maybe Sky doesn't even feel that way about me anymore," I offered.

Charlie *rolled* his eyes. "I remember that crush. It was strong. I saw him in your arms tonight."

I scoffed. "He was exhausted and cold and scared. That meant nothing." I couldn't help but recall how good Sky had felt in my arms, though.

"You won't go after him?" Charlie asked.

"Damn, man, you make me sound like a fucking predator." I was actually kinda offended.

"Van, I've watched you zero in on a guy and have him in your bed within twenty-four hours. I know how you work."

"*Charlie*, I watched you zero in on Kendall and bring her home that very same night. How is that any different? Don't go acting like you're all innocent."

"Kendall wasn't your sister," Charlie huffed.

"And if she was? You wouldn't have gone after her?" I pressed.

Charlie groaned. "Let's talk to Sky. Figure out our plan. And go from there. Just please don't take advantage of him, hurt him, or break his heart."

I stood. "I'm going to leave before either of us says something we might regret—in your case, might regret *more* —and we'll talk to Sky in the morning. Sky and I were friends before anything. That's where we'll naturally go back to, I'm sure." I paused with my hand on the door. "But I won't lose out on something that might be really great for Sky or me just because you're bent out of shape over it. This is all completely hypothetical and I get that. But *if*, somewhere down the road, something was to grow between Sky and me —or me and *any* guy—I won't let you stand in the way of my happiness. That's not what friends—not what *brothers*—do. And that's not you, Charlie."

I drove home feeling prickly and frustrated. The nerve of my best friend basically forbidding me to date his brother. *Do you have plans to date his brother?* I thumped the steering wheel. That wasn't the point. The *point* was that Charlie couldn't tell me who I could or couldn't like or date or fuck. Just because Sky was his brother didn't give Charlie the right to insinuate I had a bit of a slutty streak or that I wouldn't treat Sky right.

"Fuuuuck," I drawled as I blew out a breath. "Stop getting yourself all worked up about something that likely won't even happen. Skyler has probably completely outgrown that childish crush. He's just out of a bad relationship—hell, he may not even be *out* of it—he's probably not even thinking about jumping into something new."

I entered the house as quietly as possible, got ready for bed, found myself listening outside Sky's door like a total creeper, and then crawled into bed for one of the worst night's sleep of my entire life. And I'd slept on the rock floor of a cave once.

Fuck. I'd been serious about having no issue with Sky moving in. I'd had no issue with Sky showing up—in fact, I'd been happy to see him and thrilled Charlie got his brother back. But the chaos the day had thrown my head and heart into? Yeah, I wasn't liking that much at all.

THREE

SKYLER

I WOKE to the smell of coffee and food. My stomach growled and I glanced around the tiny room in confusion. Then the night before came rushing back to me and I groaned.

Was I stupid for coming to Charlie's? Would he be willing to let me stay? He and Van had both indicated I was welcome and that they'd actually been waiting on me to show up.

I wasn't sure how I felt about that. Were they waiting on me to show up because they'd been *so smart* and known Trent and I wouldn't work out? Or were they waiting on me to show up because they simply wanted me with them?

Charlie and Van had always been a pair. Yeah, I was the squeaky little third wheel in their friendship a lot of the time when we were younger. But did they both really want me around as much as they insinuated? Or was it just a hero complex where they both thought they could *save* me?

I growled and buried my head in the pillow. I mean, they'd bought a house with a spare room just for me according to Van. That had to mean something, right?

But I hated the thought of coming crawling back with my

tail between my legs like some little kid who couldn't make it on his own.

You would have been making it just fine on your own if not for Trent.

I sighed. I'd thought I'd loved Trent. He was the first guy I'd ever let myself fall for and I had truly thought it was going to be all sunshine and roses. Then he changed.

Did he really change or did you just finally open your eyes?

Closing my eyes, I rested my forearms over my face. Fine. Trent had been just nice enough to lure me in and then he let his true colors show through. But by that time, I was out of luck for living on campus. Couldn't pay rent on my own—and still keep up with classes. So, I was stuck.

And you convinced yourself you were happy and it wasn't so bad.

In truth, I'd also convinced myself that I couldn't do any better. What was that saying? *Better the devil you know than the devil you don't.* With Trent, I maybe wasn't sublimely happy, but I wasn't having to navigate the dating scene. I wasn't having to deal with admitting I was wrong. I wasn't having to struggle to find someone who liked me.

Terrible reasons to stay in a relationship, I knew that. But it was easier. And less scary.

I rolled from bed and took a quick shower. I didn't care to put Charlie's clothes back on since I'd been clean when I put them on, but I opted out of underwear. Today, I *had* to get to the house and get my clothes and belongings. I wondered if the guys would go with me. I wasn't looking forward to facing Trent. If I was lucky, I could time it so he wasn't there, but I'd never seemed to be lucky when it came to Trent.

I padded down the hallway and marveled at how immediately *at home* I felt in Charlie and Van's place. Yeah, there was a bit of awkwardness and some tension, but that was likely to be expected with the way I'd shown up out of the blue. But I didn't feel like an intruder; it was as if I was just a long-lost friend who'd finally returned to the fold.

I snorted. Good to see the dramatic side of me hadn't been lost.

When I turned the corner to the kitchen, I froze. Van Badger had always been bigger than me when we were younger. Taller and broader. Not fat, but beefier than me. He'd always been a protector, a caregiver, and I always thought of him as my gentle giant. None of that had changed. But *holy fuck*, Van was a fine wine and had *definitely* gotten better with age. He stood at the stove, his bare back to me, a pair of flannel pants barely hanging onto his hips. I was a respectable 5'9" and wouldn't have described myself as scrawny. But compared to Van, I looked like a short string bean. Last night when he'd hugged me, my head had fit perfectly under his chin and those broad shoulders had engulfed me in such a warm embrace that I yearned to feel it again.

Dear God, did I make some sort of moaning sound? I must have because Van turned around. The dark blond hair on his chest matched the hair on his head and the scruff on his face. His blue eyes sparkled and a smile filled his face.

And I felt as if I'd been punched in the stomach. How long had it been since someone had been glad to see me? Well, aside from my Kindergarteners, they were *always* happy to see me. His smile took my breath away and I fought hard to keep from throwing myself into his arms.

"Good morning." Van's voice was morning-rough. "Coffee is ready and I was in the mood for French toast. You want some?"

I swallowed thickly and nodded. "Yeah, sounds good." I walked to the counter and pulled a coffee mug from the cabinet. "Coffee smells good. Is it the kind you use at Byrd and Badger?"

Van turned a questioning look my way. "We don't do coffee."

I raised a brow. "Oh, my bad. I guess when I see *brew* I think of coffee as much as beer."

Van pursed his lips and was silent for a moment. "We do our own beer and cider. Plus, we sell local beers, ciders, and liquors." He appeared to be thinking deeply. "But you know what? That's a fucking brilliant idea. Coffee, tea, brunch type stuff in the morning; beer, ciders, bar food in the afternoon and evening." He dropped the spatula and wrapped me in a surprising hug. "You're a damn genius," he mumbled into the top of my head.

Without thought, I slipped my arms around his waist and melted into the hug. Trent had never been super big on physical affection unless he was in the mood for me to suck his dick or he wanted to fuck me. I'd soooo missed hugs and kisses. I cleared my throat at the thought of kissing Van. Yeah, probably not the best way to start the new roommate situation. I'd settle for the hug. "Um, your toast might need to be turned," I suggested.

Van startled and released me to flip the bread in the frying pan. "Sorry, got a little excited for a second." He cleared his throat.

My cheeks heated. "I didn't mind. Just didn't want you to burn my breakfast." I winked. "So, would it be easy to add the morning idea to the business?"

Van nodded. "I think so. Charlie would have to work through the numbers and details and such—he's the business mind—but I can't see any reason we wouldn't want to add that. I can't believe we've never thought of it."

"Where is Charlie?" I asked as I sipped the delicious coffee.

Van sat two plates of French toast on the table and

gestured for me to join him. "He went to work to get some things done. Then he wants us all to talk."

I groaned.

Van laughed. "You know he's not going to let things go without a discussion. Charlie Byrd doesn't work that way."

"I know," I mumbled around a bite of deliciousness. "I just hate how lame it's all going to make me sound. And admitting I'm wrong isn't a strong suit for me." I wrinkled my nose.

Van laughed. "It never was." He took a bite. "Charlie isn't here to rub things in your face. He just wants to know you're okay. He's scared you're going to leave again. He really wants you here with us."

I shook my head and took a sip of my coffee. "*Why*? Why would he want me here after the way I acted?"

Van smiled softly. "He loves you and he's missed you like crazy. You guys were close growing up, you stayed close when he went off to college—maybe more so since I was gone—and he was pretty devastated when you shut them out."

I sighed and dipped my head feeling guilty and broken-hearted.

"Look, it's just a talk. I don't think Charlie plans to berate you or interrogate you. I think he's more interested in letting you know you've got a place here and making plans for the future." Van took the last bite of his breakfast and washed it down with coffee.

"Why do I get the feeling I'm being talked about?" Charlie asked as he sauntered into the kitchen.

"Because you *are* and because you're a nosy motherfucker," Van deadpanned. "Let me clean this up. I'll meet you guys in the living room. Skyler just gave me an amazing idea for Byrd and Badger."

Charlie cocked a brow. "Helping with the business already, huh?"

My cheeks pinked and I shrugged. "Just assumed something and it gave Van an idea." I glanced to where Van was rinsing dishes before putting them in the dishwasher. "You need help?"

"Nah, just going to start the washer. I'll be there in five minutes."

So strange to eat a meal and not be told it was automatically my job to clean the mess. I didn't mind the set-up of *I cook, you clean*, but Trent never allowed me to cook. He always said my cooking was dangerous and wasteful. So, I was relegated to the one *always* cleaning—and he made such a huge mess; it was like he purposefully made the biggest amount of dirty dishes possible to make sure I had to do them. And then he'd stand there and nit-pick my every move as I cleaned them up. Which usually ended in me getting upset and yelling. Then he'd tell me to relax, I was being too sensitive, and he was *just joking*. Yeah well, it's only a joke if both sides think it's funny.

I poured more coffee after Charlie had made himself a cup, then I followed him to the living room and we sat on the couch. Not gonna lie; I kinda felt like a kid in the principal's office.

"I see the crush on Van hasn't really faded," Charlie murmured before sipping his coffee.

My ears caught fire. "What?" I sputtered.

"Dude, you've had a crush on him since you were ten."

"You *knew*?" I asked.

Charlie snorted. "Anyone who spent more than five minutes around you knew. You had it bad for six long years." He took another drink and eyed me over his mug. "And it either never ended or it's come rushing back."

I shrugged. "Doesn't matter." The attraction was *definitely* still there, but I couldn't let that cause a problem.

"Look, I'm just saying I don't think he's your type."
Charlie shifted.

"Um, yeah, I get it. I'm not the type to go after straight
guys."

Charlie's eyes widened as if he was shocked. "Right, yeah.
I didn't think you were. Either way, it's for the best, huh?
Would be all kinds of weird and awkward. Best to just keep
the three of us as friends, yeah?"

I narrowed my eyes at Charlie. "Why are you being
weird?"

Charlie shook his head. "Nothing. So, what's this big idea
you gave Van?"

Van walked into the living room as Charlie was
speaking.

"So, Skyler is pouring himself coffee and asks if it's the
same stuff we use at Byrd and Badger," Van starts. "I tell him
we don't do coffee and he frowns."

I interjected. "I just think of coffee and tea when I hear
the word brew."

Charlie's eyes darted between me and Van for a moment
before he smiled and gave a little whoop. "Hot damn, you
coming home has more than one benefit. That's a great
idea!" He reached over and smacked the back of my head.
"Good job, Squirt."

"Oh God, please don't call me that." I buried my head in
my hands. "You know I hate when you call me that."

Charlie laughed. "You're staying, right? With us? You're
not going back?"

My head jerked up as I tried to follow the conversation.
"Whoa, change of topic much?"

"Sorry, I want to hear what brought you here, but more
than anything, I just want to know you're staying." Charlie's
eyes bore into mine and I saw Van smile from his place in the
nearby recliner.

"Yeah, if you'll have me, I'm staying. Maybe not forever. I'm sure you don't want me here forever."

"Why not?" Charlie scowled.

"I mean, you're getting married. I'm sure your new wife would like to eventually have a place of her own." Then a thought entered my head. "Oh God, is this like a throuple? I didn't even think about that." My eyes darted between Van and Charlie.

Van threw his head back and laughed and Charlie joined in.

When they'd both settled down and wiped tears from their eyes, Charlie spoke. "No, Kendall and I are just a couple. We don't have a third or an open relationship."

My eyes grew wide. "Wow, I'm kinda amazed you even know about that."

My brother scoffed. "I'm not a fucking homophobe or transphobe. Or any kinda of phobe—okay, I don't love spiders and snakes, but like I don't have issues with any types of relationships or love as long as it's consensual."

"Then why did you get so upset over me being gay?" I asked the question even though, in my heart, I knew it wasn't really fair.

"Sky, I know you have a very hard time admitting you were wrong, but I really need you to think back to that day."

I bristled.

"I'm not going to nag or put you down or rub it in, nothing like that. Just think about it. First, I'd known you were gay since you were about ten." He gave me a look that said *Right about the time you started crushing on my best friend.* "Mom and Dad knew…"

"What?" I croaked. "Why didn't anyone say anything?"

"Mom and Dad said we needed to let you come to things by yourself and just be supportive. Looking back, I wish we'd done it differently. At least, I wish *I'd* done it differently.

Maybe I should have let you know that I'd always support you no matter what." Charlie ran a hand over his face. "Instead, we come to pack your dorm room up. It's fucking hotter than Hades. We're all about to pass out from lack of food. The damn water fountain water is lukewarm at best. The elevators aren't working and we're carrying a damn mini-fridge down the stairs when you come stalking up with that asshole. *This is Trent. He's my boyfriend. Yes, I'm gay. You either deal with it or lose me.*" My brother narrowed his eyes. "I want you to think very carefully about that day. What did the three of us say and do when you introduced Trent and said you were gay?"

I started to argue. I wanted to protest. I wanted to be right. But I glanced at Van and saw his supportive, kind smile and I froze. I made myself really think back to that day. Clearing my throat, I spoke softly, "You slapped me on the back and said you loved me." Tears stung my eyes. "Dad gave me a nod as he continued wrestling the fridge. Mom gave me a sweaty hug and told me she loved me. She smiled at Trent and said it was nice to meet him." A tear slipped from the corner of my eye. "But then it all went to hell."

Charlie smiled sadly. "What made it go to hell?"

I closed my eyes and wiped at the tears before pinching the bridge of my nose. "Trent. He was yelling at me. Called me names. Was rude to Mom and Dad. Nearly had a fight with you. And then he refused to let me go with you all to eat dinner." God, had I really lost my parents and brother over Trent? Had I really chosen such an asshole over my good, loving, supportive family?

"We pulled you aside and said we didn't like the way Trent was treating you. We asked you to come home with us," Charlie's words were soft.

I sighed. "And I flipped the fuck out like the drama queen that I am. Accused you of being homophobic and not accepting me." Another tear fell down my face. These were things I'd recently started to admit to myself—the worse Trent got, the more I could admit that my family really hadn't been the problem—but saying the words out loud was a slap in the face.

"Look, I'm not trying to upset you," Charlie began, "I just need you to know that Mom and Dad and I *never* sent you away or didn't accept you. We have always and will always be your biggest supports."

"Me, too," Van chimed in.

"I don't know how I let myself get so lost. I've always hated feeling like I need others or can't handle something on my own. I guess I wanted to play the part of a grown-up so badly that I used your dislike of Trent to convince myself you didn't want me because I was gay. I was going to prove I could be on my own; prove I didn't need anyone." I dropped my chin to my chest. "And here I am with a black eye, nowhere to live, dragging my tail between my legs."

"Fuck that," Van growled. "A real man accepts help and knows his family and friends love him."

I closed my eyes and tried to believe him. "It's just hard. I've had it in my mind for so long that needing help or coming home meant failure."

Charlie grunted. "When have Mom or Dad ever made it seem like that?"

I waved a hand. "Not *them*, just society. I didn't want to become that sad Kindergarten teacher in his early thirties still living in his parents' basement."

"One, you're far from thirty. Two, Mom and Dad don't have a basement. If anything, they'd let you have the den if Mom hasn't left your room exactly the same. Three, you teach Kindergarten?" Charlie's eyes sparkled.

I rolled my eyes. "Details," I said dismissing his first two points. "I don't have my teaching license yet. I'm in my final semester. But I'm doing my student teaching with Kindergarten and I love it."

"That's amazing. I don't know how you have the patience for it."

Van shivered. "Way too much snot and germs for me."

I laughed. "They're amazing. Even on my worst days, they make me smile. I love teaching and I love my babies." I took a deep breath. "But student teaching is one of my biggest issues. I can't work more than maybe an hour or so a day and a bit on weekends. I've got lesson plans, grading, planning meetings for school *and* all the coursework still for the college. No one wants to hire me for an hour an evening and six hours on the weekend." I grimaced. "Trent had told me from the beginning—*if* he let me stick around that long—that he'd cover rent this semester. But he, of course, squanders money like nobody's business so he was always short on rent and then would take it out on me."

Fury rippled off both Charlie and Van. I could physically feel their anger.

"No, no, not like that. This," I pointed to my eye, "was the first time he ever hit me. I'm not proud of the shit I put up with until that point, but I'm also not going to be the type that goes back to someone who would hit me. I'm done."

My brother and Van both sagged as if a huge weight had been lifted from them.

"My biggest issue right now is lack of money and getting back to the house to get all of my stuff without Trent causing a huge scene." I winced. "And he tracks my phone so he likely knows where I'm at."

Charlie gritted his teeth. "Okay, so here's the plan. You don't worry about rent until you graduate and get a job."

"Charlie, I can't do that. I'd feel like a charity case."

"So, you'd let Asshole cover your rent and treat you like

shit, but you won't let your family cover you and support you as you finish this semester?"

I sighed. I knew my brother—even after all of this time—there was no arguing with him.

"You can work an hour or so at Byrd and Badger on evenings when you've got time. And weekends we can use you as many hours as you've got to give. Your pay won't be what others are making, but you can keep tips and we'll pay enough that you'll have a bit of cash. Working for us will cover your rent and groceries. At least until you get a job." Charlie nodded as he agreed with himself on his declaration. "We'll go with you to the house. I'd like to see Asshat *try* to cause an issue."

I chuckled. Charlie was built much more like Van than like me. They made an imposing pair.

"And we'll get you a new phone. First thing is the phone. We'll transfer any of the info to the new one and then you can leave the old one at the house for Trent."

I pursed my lips. "I kinda feel guilty leaving Trent alone with the bills and shit."

"Were you paying anything right now?" Charlie asked.

I shook my head. "No, that was the agreement. I'd take this semester to just get through student teaching and he'd cover it all."

"Then no reason to feel guilty. He doesn't have money? His fault, not yours," my brother growled.

I took a deep breath and nodded.

"Okay, so Byrd and Badger is covered today. We're taking a road trip. Walmart first for underwear. I have no issues with you wearing my clothes, but I'm drawing the line at underwear."

I laughed as I examined the clothes I'd borrowed. "Not to mention that these are falling off me."

"Can't help you're smaller than me, Squirt," Charlie teased and I groaned.

"Okay, Walmart and phone. Then we fortify with lunch and square off at the house. Sound like a plan?" Van asked with an excited smile.

"We may luck out and get there when Trent isn't home," I suggested.

Van wrinkled his nose. "Where's the fun in that?"

I laughed.

WALMART TURNED out to be a lot of fun. It had been ages since I'd been able to just be silly and let loose. That sounds ridiculous, I know. I was twenty-four years old and I hadn't had fun in Walmart in ages? Well, since BT—before Trent.

Trent never let me do the grocery shopping. Said I didn't know the right quality of foods to buy. *Whatever, bitch. We're shopping at Walmart; is true quality really an issue?* Plus, he hated if I bought something that wasn't on the list. But of course, he could buy anything he decided he needed. But if I bought something as a splurge or just to try something new, he gave me shit for days. That was the thing about Trent—or at least one of the things about him—he could hold a grudge forever. Fights were never just about the issue at hand; he *always* brought up old shit from months ago.

Anyway, Walmart with Charlie and Van was fun. After grabbing a few dry goods and toiletries, we ended up in the clothing section. Charlie was perusing socks, but Van was teasing me in the underwear section.

"Ohhh, string bikinis? Who knew Wally World had such kinky options. I mean, who wouldn't want to wear these?" Van held up a package of underwear.

"Me," I laughed. "I definitely wouldn't want to wear those."

"Don't like them skimpy?"

I started to blush and protest, but cocked my head to the side. If I was going to be starting over and living with Van and Charlie, I could start over as myself. "Oh, I like skimpy, just not Walmart skimpy."

Van's cheeks pinked. "More of a Target guy?" he sputtered.

I wasn't the type to *try* to make a straight guy feel uncomfortable—unless of course he was being homophobic, then I'd lay it on thick—but Van was a friend so I knew I could mess with him. "I'm a varied type of guy. Some days I like loose boxer shorts." I wrinkled my nose. "Okay, that actually doesn't happen all that often. Too bunchy. But I digress. I usually go for a good solid pair of boxer briefs or hipster briefs—just a little classier than whitey-tighties." I moved closer to Van and bit my lip. "But you never know which days will find me in a jock or a pair of skimpy, silky panties."

I swear to God, Van almost choked on his tongue. He hung the package back on the rack and mumbled something about needing to find the restroom.

I couldn't help but laugh at his retreating back. Straight guys were so easy. I mean, really? The image of a guy in silk panties was *that* much of a turn-off that he couldn't even finish the conversation? Classic.

I was actually looking forward to getting my clothes from Trent's because I was ready to start wearing my sexy underwear again. Trent always made me feel less or dirty for it—but of course he got off on it when he'd make me wear the silky panties when he felt like using me for a fuck-hole—and I'd eventually just stopped wearing the sexy ones in favor of boring cotton hipsters or boxer briefs. But with Trent out of the picture—I scoffed inwardly because I knew he'd never be out of the picture *that* easily—I was excited to get back to being me. I smiled sadly as I threw a couple packages into the cart; I hated that I'd lost *me* for a while, but I was happy to be back.

Van and Charlie found me by the t-shirts a bit later. Charlie was scowling and Van looked a bit nervous.

"So, this isn't exactly where I'd planned to do this," Charlie began. He gestured toward Van. "But you seem to have rendered him incapable of anything but pathetic grunts and frustrated sighs, so this is as good as anywhere. I wasn't asking him to hide anything or lie." Charlie glared. "I swear, I wasn't." He glanced at his feet and shuffled a bit. "I realize that not every gay guy finds every other gay guy attractive. I realize that you two may not click beyond friendship. And Dear God, *please*, that's how I want it to play out. Can't we just be friends? Please don't put me in the middle of whatever and then expect me to pick sides when it crashes and burns. He's not been the most discerning and you've been through a bad relationship. Let's just be friends, please?"

Van scowled. "Hey, I'm always safe."

My brother shrugged. "He's my brother."

I stared at Charlie for so long he finally took the three shirts I was holding in my hands and tossed them into the cart. "Sky? You good?"

I swallowed. Hard. And attempted to process what my brother had said. "Wait, what?" was all I could muster.

"I'm gay," Van offered. "I didn't think it was going to be a big deal, but dumbass here thinks it's like the beginning of the end."

"I don't think your sexuality is the beginning of the end," Charlie groused. He shrugged petulantly. "I just don't want either of you hurt or me having to take a side."

When what I was hearing finally began to sink in, I couldn't help but grin. "I have soooo many questions," I spoke directly to Van and then winked. This could be fun in a variety of ways. Especially if it meant giving Charlie a hard time. "But we should probably fuck each other's brains out all over the house—you know how the gays are—just to be sure we do or don't like each other."

Van threw his head back and laughed.

Charlie groaned.

And I chuckled. I still thought Van was hot as hell. I was *very* intrigued that he'd been "straight" when he left to travel the world and now he was gay—or now he was admitting or accepting or *whatever* that he was gay. I really did have a lot of questions. But I wasn't stupid enough to think that just because we were both gay we'd end up happily ever after. And I respected myself and my brother and Van enough to not fuck things up with a one-night-stand. Was a one-night-stand even possible when the hookup was your roommate?

I wasn't at all against something happening between me and Van, but I knew it would be something that was gradual, more than just a hookup. And I did kinda see what Charlie was saying. It would be hard for him to be in the middle if things with me and Van crashed and burned. So, I'd go into this new living situation with my eyes wide open. I'd be grateful to have my brother and Van supporting me. And if something happened with Van that turned our friendship into something more, then so be it. But I wasn't going to go seeking it.

A thought hit me like a ton of bricks. Did Van bring dates or boyfriends or hookups home? My gut clenched. I'd have to be okay with it. But a green-eyed monster was definitely raring to go.

We left Walmart and headed toward the phone store.

"Wanna do drinks and talk tonight?" Van asked quietly as

we walked toward the store. "Just us? Figure we have a lot to talk about."

I glanced ahead where Charlie was stalking toward the store on a mission and nodded. "Yeah, I'd like that."

Van gave my shoulder a squeeze and I smiled. Suddenly, the whole shitty situation from the day before was looking a lot brighter thanks to Charlie and Van. Skyler Byrd was possibly knocked down, but he wasn't out. I was a fighter and I'd get back up and keep going. I had no doubt.

FOUR

VAN

I FELT BETTER KNOWING that Skyler knew I was gay. I kinda understood Charlie's point, but I'd promised I'd never hide the real me, so keeping it from Sky wasn't sitting right.

"So, how did you and Kendall meet?" Skyler asked as we munched on an appetizer platter at a local restaurant.

Charlie took a sip of soda. "Oh, um," he stuttered, "party at Byrd and Badger. I was working, she was there with friends."

I laughed. "What he's not telling you is that it was meant to be a one-night-stand, and they've been together ever since."

Skyler gaped. "*You?*" He pretended to be shocked. "My brother? Charlie Byrd? The no-nonsense, everything-planned-to-the-last-detail, sensible to his dying breath, Charlie Byrd was going to have a one-night-stand?"

Charlie snorted. "Didn't exactly go as planned. We kinda connected on a different level than anyone I've ever met. She's pretty damn perfect." His eyes got all soft and sparkly.

"Awww, Charlie's in love," Sky teased.

I smiled. I loved to give Charlie a rough time about how

quickly he fell head over heels for Kendall, but I also adored seeing him so happy. "Kendall is the yin to Charlie's yang; they really balance each other out. She's good people."

Skyler ate a potato skin and sucked his bottom lip in before allowing his eyes to flutter to mine. "And you? Have your perfect match?"

Charlie groaned.

Fuck. Why did Skyler have to be so damn cute?

And why did he have to tell me about his jocks and God damned silk panties? I was *never* going to get the image of Skyler in a skimpy pair of silk panties out of my head.

I gritted my teeth. "Nah, haven't found the right person just yet."

"Not for lack of trying," Charlie interjected. "Our dear Van came home from traveling abroad, told me he was gay, and proceeded to hook up with nearly every male in a fifty-mile-radius."

I scoffed. "It wasn't that bad. Plus, I'm safe. What's wrong with having a little fun? This way, I'll know when the right guy comes along because I've already gone through all the wrong ones." I couldn't help but glance at Sky. Something stirred in my gut when his big brown eyes met mine.

Skyler smiled. "Sounds like me once I got to college. I'd known I was gay since I was ten."

Charlie snorted. "Yeah, we all knew."

"I still don't get why you guys didn't just tell me," Sky said, tossing a fry at his head.

Charlie shrugged. "Mom said it wasn't our place to tell you what we thought you were and we just had to be patient until you were ready to tell us."

"Yeah, I can see that. Can even appreciate it. But it kinda backfired because I got it in my head—not from anything you all did, just my crazy head—that I couldn't tell you. So, I hid it until I got to college. Then I got a little taste of freedom and I fucked everything with a heartbeat." Sky's eyes grew wide and he clamped a hand over his mouth. "Oh my God, that sounded terrible hearing it out loud. I wasn't *that* bad. And I was always safe. I made out with *a lot* of guys. Messed around with quite a few. Actually had sex with a couple handfuls." His forehead crinkled. "Then I met Trent and it all went to hell."

I wanted to reach over and take his hand and give it a squeeze, but I controlled myself.

"Can I ask what the hell you saw in that asshole?" Charlie asked as our food was put on the table.

Sky took a bite of his chicken sandwich. "Looking back? I really have no clue. I mean, he's this big, burly guy so maybe it was a protection thing. But he really let himself go after we got together. He treated me really nice when we first met. Showered me with attention and gifts. I fell for it—and feel really shallow for it now. I think the main thing was the draw of living off campus and being so grown-up. Setting up house, proving myself. But as soon as we moved in, Trent changed. Constantly reminding me that the house was his, I didn't have any legal right to it. What I'd thought was going to be a relationship and partnership quickly turned into Trent expecting me to be at his beck and call for cleaning, paying bills, and sex."

My fucking teeth were going to be ground to nubs by the time I heard this whole story.

Charlie's glare was intense, but he encouraged his brother to continue.

Sky took another bite and washed it down with soda.

I'd noticed his ears had pinked.

"Trent was an exclusive top," he said in a quiet voice so as not to draw the attention of our fellow diners. "Something he let me know often. When we'd get in fights, he'd constantly bring up sex-related things. *You used to be all about sucking my dick; couldn't keep you off it. Now you turn your nose up like it's a chore.* He acted like he was the king and should be celebrated if he ever deemed it acceptable to blow me." Skyler shrugged. "I'm not saying I wanted to top all the time," he whispered and my gut stirred with thoughts of Skyler top, bottom, whichever way I could get him.

So, Sky shows up and you—for the first time in your life—have a crush? A love at first sight type thing? I pushed the thought away; I'd always loved Sky as a friend and little brother. A crush? Nah, just glad to have him around again.

Charlie—God, I loved that man—had the good sense to listen to his brother talk about sexual positions as if it was something he discussed every day. He nodded and just listened.

"But the few times I'd hint around that maybe we could switch things up, Trent would go ballistic. Screaming that he wasn't that type and if I thought he was bending over for anyone—especially a twink like me—I needed to think again." He closed his eyes. "I put up with his shit for three years. I'm embarrassed that it took a punch to the face to wake me up."

"You really didn't see it?" I asked.

Sky started to shake his head, but he stopped and put his chin down. "No, I saw it. I recognized it—not in the very beginning, but within a year or less. But I needed a place to live. No way I could student teach and pay for an apartment. I was just stuck." He sighed. "I should have left way back in the beginning and gotten a job so I could be prepared for this last semester. But way back then I kept telling myself he'd change."

Charlie grunted. "Mom and Dad and I were there, the whole time, we would have helped."

Sky smiled sadly. "Are you forgetting my dramatic, stubborn streak? No way."

"What changed when he hit you?" I asked quietly.

He took a deep breath. "I guess I'd never seen myself as an abuse victim—although, I would have told anyone else in my position to get out—*until* the physical abuse started. Trent begged and sobbed while I grabbed my stuff. If he'd hit me at the beginning, I likely would have stayed. But I'd had three years of his shit and the fist was the last straw. He was yelling that it was my fault by the time I walked out the door, but I didn't even look back."

I couldn't help it. I placed a hand on his leg under the table. "None of what he did was ever your fault."

Sky glanced at my hand on his leg, bit his lip as his eyes met mine, and nodded. "I know. I just hate that I lost so much time. Nearly lost my family because of him."

Charlie huffed. "Three years is nothing in the grand scheme of things. You're here now and we're going to fix it. Your family is here for you. And some day, when you meet the guy who deserves you, we'll support you in that too. I'm sorry things with Trent got so bad," Charlie said before pausing.

"Is this where you tell me that you were right, you all tried to tell me I was making a mistake? Are you going to hang this over my head for the rest of my days?" Sky joked.

Charlie pinched the bridge of his nose. "No, but Mom and Dad are going to fucking *kill* me. I can't believe I haven't thought to tell them you're here."

Skyler's eyes went wide. "Oh, shit. I didn't even think about it." He took a deep breath. "You really think they'll be okay with everything?"

I interrupted. "No doubt in my mind. They accepted me without even a blink of an eye. They'll be so thrilled to know you're back."

"I know this sounds terrible, but can we wait until tomorrow? I want to get my clothes and stuff and then settle in. I've got school work to do." Sky glanced my way. "And some other stuff."

My stomach clenched. Had I ever been that excited about *just a drink* with *just a friend*?

"Tomorrow, I'll make sure all of my stuff for Monday is done by noon. Then we can spend the rest of the day with Mom and Dad." Sky wrinkled his nose. "As bad as it sounds, it's been three years. Surely twenty-four hours won't be that much of a problem."

"Easy for you to say. Once they find out you ended up on my porch last night and I didn't call them until Sunday? I'm dead meat." Charlie ran a hand through his hair.

"I'll tell them I needed time to settle in and process. It's not a total lie," Sky quipped.

We finished our lunch and headed toward Trent's place.

"God, I hope he's not home," Sky muttered.

"Nah, I think it will be best if he sees you taking your things and gets the picture that it's done, over, finished," I said. I was so ready to push my fist through Trent's face.

"He's going to get so ugly," Skyler warned.

"That's fine. We've dealt with ugly at Byrd and Badger. Trent may have some pounds on us, but we're taller and better built. He doesn't sound as if he's been using his bulk for anything good lately," Charlie groused.

"He wouldn't know a bench press if it bitch-slapped him," Sky deadpanned. "That's really not fair of me, but he stopped any and all kind of effort to keep himself in shape the moment I moved in. That probably sounds shallow, but between his attitude and the abuse, I lost any and all attraction to him. He will be scared of the two of you being with me. He doesn't do well with confrontation."

"Just likes to pick on the little guy with no backup," I growled.

"Pretty much." Skyler groaned. "Shit, he's home."

We pulled up to a small white house that looked very similar to the surrounding homes. All of them had been built when the college had first been erected and they'd seen years and years of students, faculty, and college employees living in them.

"Let's keep it civil. We don't get nasty no matter how bad Trent gets," I offered. "We all in agreement on that?" I didn't want to run Sky through the wringer, and Charlie and I had our business to think of.

Charlie and Skyler nodded.

"Let's have some fun," I said with a waggle of my brow.

Charlie and Sky both chuckled at my excitement.

"Go on," I urged Sky. "We're right behind you." I had a feeling Sky needed to feel in control of this, but there was no way Charlie and I weren't going to be by his side.

Sky climbed from the car and made his way toward the door.

Trent threw open the door, a smug sneer on his face, and a nasty laugh. He crossed his arms and blocked the entrance with his large frame.

Charlie went to exit the car, but I stopped him. "Hold up, let's give it a minute." I was dying to go slam my fist into Trent's mouth, but I didn't think he'd noticed we were in the car just yet and I wanted to see what he was going to do or say before we let our presence be known.

"So, the little bitch comes crawling back home, huh? Get your ass in the house and don't even think about pulling a stunt like that again," Trent demanded.

Glancing at each other with a matching *Oh, fuck, no he didn't* looks, Charlie and I climbed from the car slowly and walked to stand behind Sky as Trent's eyes grew wide and his skin paled.

Sky's shoulders straightened as if our being behind him

gave him the boost of courage he'd been looking for. "Just here to get my things. We won't take long."

"Brought some goons to do your fighting, huh?" Trent sneered and eyed Charlie and me.

"No fighting necessary," Sky answered calmly. "Would you rather I'd brought the police? Because I can."

Trent narrowed his eyes. "I don't know what shit you think you're taking." He jutted his chin. "House is mine. Makes everything in it mine."

"Just want my clothes and makeup; nothing you'd have any use for." Sky took a step closer.

Trent continued to block the door.

Charlie and I moved closer.

Trent glared, but he moved to the side. "Make it quick."

"I'd like you and the guys to all watch me as I throw stuff in bags. I don't want it said that I took anything that wasn't mine," Sky said as he walked into the house.

"Better yet," Charlie said jovially, "I'll video it so there are no mistakes made."

I knew he was thinking Trent would try to say Sky stole from him. I knew because Charlie was my best friend and I was thinking the exact same thing.

Trent stood with his arms crossed and shot daggers at Sky.

Sky grabbed four duffle bags from his closet. "You'll agree that all four of these bags are mine, yes?"

Trent nodded.

Charlie swung his phone toward Trent. "Can you say that out loud? Are those four bags Skyler's?"

"Yes," Trent huffed.

Within twenty minutes, Skyler had emptied his side of the closet and his dresser drawers into two of the bags, piled his shoes into a third, and dumped his makeup bags and boxes into the fourth duffel. He grabbed his toothbrush, a comb, some hair products, and a small bottle of cologne.

"I think that's it," Sky said to Charlie.

"You have all your school supplies? Computer? Charger?" Charlie asked.

Sky nodded. "That was all in my backpack. Oh, I do have a box of school stuff."

"Let me take these out to the car. I'll be back for the box," I offered.

Sky smiled softly at me. "Thanks."

By the time I packed the car, they were all outside. Charlie took the box to the car and I stepped close to stand behind Sky.

"I know the phone was yours and on your plan, so I won't be needing it," Sky said as he handed his old phone to a shocked and angry-looking Trent—I really don't think the man thought Skyler had it in him to leave. "I've got a new number, so this is a good time for both of us to make a clean break. I'm really sorry things went the way they did."

I grunted.

"Not that I'm saying things going the way they did was my fault. I'm just sad we ended up in this situation. But I think it may be for the best. I wish you well, Trent." Sky took a tiny step backward and his back pressed against my chest.

"So, your slutty little bottom-boy ass already went hunting for the next dick you could find? Got him to take pity on you? You work quick. Pathetic." Scorn and hatred dripped from Trent's words.

Without a second thought, I wrapped an arm around Sky's chest—and smiled inside at his breathy gasp—and kissed the top of his head instinctively. "What we have is built on a lifetime of love and respect. He's found someone who supports him and would *never* hurt him. Someone who would never treat him as just a piece of ass."

Trent's tomato-red face contorted as he spat, "Yeah well, have fun with that. You may think you've found the perfect little cock sucker, but soon he'll lose his enthusiasm. Let me know how loving and supportive you're feeling when little twinky bottom-boy decides he wants to go all vers on you." Trent curled his nose. "That's not the way the game is played; I didn't sign up for that."

"I'll be so busy sucking him and spreading my legs for his gorgeous cock, I wouldn't even know what you're talking about," I replied with a wink. "Come on, babe. Let's go home." I made a show of nuzzling Sky's ear before turning the two of us, taking his hand, and walking to the car.

"That was pretty amazing—a bit over the top, but amazing all the same." Charlie laughed as we got into the car.

"Is he watching?" I asked.

Charlie cast a quick glance toward Trent. "Yep."

"Good." I said with a contented smile.

We drove off and as soon as we were around the corner, Sky moaned from the back seat. "Oh my God, that was tense. Van, did you take drama classes on your travels? You totally didn't have to do that, but you played it so perfectly."

I shrugged. "It wasn't a total lie. You and I do have a relationship built on love and respect—being friends since you were born will do that to people. I do support you. And I'm vers so I'd have no problem with my guy wanting to top whenever the mood struck."

Sky made some sort of strangled noise from the back seat.

Charlie groaned.

And I laughed. Laughing was the only way I could hope to make my head and dick stop thinking about making that entire scene we just played out for Trent actually come true.

FIVE

SKYLER

MY BELLY WAS STILL aflutter hours after the standoff with Trent. Partly because I'd been so nervous and I was damn relieved I'd been able to get my belongings with very little drama.

Mostly because of Van. In my mind, I *knew* he'd been acting. But my heart wanted to believe otherwise. When he'd wrapped his arm around me and pressed his lips against my head, nothing had felt so *right* in my entire life. His words about love and respect and his easy promise to support me kept playing over and over in my head. What he'd said about sucking me and spreading his legs for me had gone straight to my dick and I couldn't stop thinking about it. *That* part of the confrontation with Trent had messed me up a lot more than the actual confrontation with Trent.

Van slid open the patio door and joined me on the little loveseat by the firepit. Kendall was out with friends and Charlie was at the bar—Van said my brother had been immersed in planning for the addition of coffee and tea.

He handed me a frosty mug. "Our most popular cider."

I took a sip. "Mmmm, that's good."

We settled in with our drinks and played catch-up as we spoke of the years Van had been overseas and I'd been at college. It was odd and very comforting how Van and I slipped into our easy, relaxed relationship so quickly. I guess that's what knowing someone since you were very young would do.

"I was so sad for you when your grandma died," I said after a sip.

Van smiled fondly. "She was an amazing woman. But her passing is what gave me the kick to leave. I'd had this strong urge to travel, see the world, find myself. I miss her every day, but I know she was proud of me and she'd be happy for me."

"So, did you know you were gay when you left home?" I thought back to that summer when Charlie headed off to college and Van left for his journey. "I was so devastated; I lost my two best friends at the same time."

Van nudged his shoulder against mine. "I'm sorry. I hated to leave, but I knew it was something I had to do." He was quiet for a moment. "I don't think I'd labeled anything at that point. I knew you had a bit of puppy-love for me," he winked, "but I wasn't sure what I was feeling—honestly, I'm glad you and I didn't experiment back then. I found girls and guys both attractive, but in different ways. It wasn't until I was trekking through mountain and forest paths on the other side of the earth that I was able to separate the feelings. My attraction to girls wasn't sexual—for a while I thought I was asexual. But the more I recognized I wasn't sexually attracted to girls, the more I had to examine that I *was* sexually attracted to guys." He chuckled. "At first, I freaked out because I wasn't sure what that would do to me and Charlie. But then I realized that there was *definitely* no sexual attraction between me and my best friend. I fooled around with a quite a few guys overseas—just to be sure," he teased.

"Then I came home, told your family, and got to work with Charlie on Byrd and Badger. Allowing myself to be the real me was one of the most freeing things I've ever done and I've never looked back."

I smiled and leaned into his shoulder. "I was about ten when I realized guys at school were talking about girls and how pretty they were—and it only got more evident to me as I got older. I liked talking to the girls about hair and makeup and movies, but I wasn't agog over the girls the way the other boys were. I was definitely more interested in the male celebrities that the girls had crushes on than the female ones the boys hung posters of in their rooms." I bit my lip. "And that was when I got stars in my eyes for you."

"Awww," Van teased.

"But for several years, I just thought I was different. I knew I liked looking at guys more than looking at girls. I knew seeing you in swim trunks gave me all kinds of butterflies. But I wasn't sure what to *do* with that information. Then you and Charlie left me and I was stuck trying to navigate the murky waters of finding myself." I took a deep breath. "I'll never really know why or how I convinced myself that telling my parents and Charlie was a bad idea. Really wish I could change that." I shrugged. "But it is what it is." I took a final swig of cider and glanced at the *six* empty mugs and cans. We'd been chatting and mindlessly drinking for nearly two hours. I shivered in the night breeze.

Van's arm went around me and I immediately melted into him. No awkwardness, no sense of *oh shit*. Just a warm, protective, comforting arm.

"This okay?" Van whispered.

I nodded against him.

"Charlie has a point," Van began as if reluctant to bring up the subject.

I sighed. "I know." I really did know that.

"But I'm not willing to pass on something that could be really great just because it puts him in a tough spot," Van continued.

"Really?" A glimmer of hope flickered in my chest.

Van's arm tightened. "Really. But I guess we've got some things to think about."

"What's that?" I whispered.

"What is this? Is it a teen crush carried over? Is it me challenging Charlie? Is it you being hurt and needing comfort and me being the type who wants to protect? Is it easy and simple or complex and complicated?" Van sighed. "All I know is, it can't be a one-off, throw away type thing. I respect both you and Charlie too much for that. And I wouldn't do that to our history—we've got too much of a past together to throw away a friendship for a one-night-stand."

I chuckled. "Not to mention it would be awkward as fuck if we're living together."

Van laughed. "Yeah, there's also that."

"I don't think my crush on you ever went away," I murmured. "The moment you opened that door, it all came crashing back." I cuddled closer. "But I'm not that young kid with starry eyes and butterflies."

Van pulled away to study my face. "I don't know, you look pretty starry-eyed to me. And no butterflies? I need to up my game."

I smiled. "Okay, definitely butterflies. But in a more grown-up sense of the word. I like you. I've always liked you. I like what you stand for, how you treat people, how you've always been this gentle-giant who cared for and protected me —I guess I'm saying I like you beyond *he's hot* now that I'm older. But I also respect Charlie and you enough to know I don't want to put any of us in an awkward position."

"So, you'd pass up on exploring whatever this could

maybe be just for Charlie?" His question held just the smallest edge of a challenge.

I shook my head. "No. But I *would* be careful, go slow, weigh the pros and cons before jumping into something. The thought of what you and I *could be* is exciting and overwhelming. But it's also crazy—I just today found out you're gay. Yes, I've had a crush on you forever, but what about how you've felt about me?"

Van nodded. "I get that. I won't lie and say I've been pining for you since the day I left. You were still a kid in my mind until you showed up at the door. Then, all the love and respect I had for you met with this crazy physical attraction and I was a goner. Never had that happen before and it's kinda messing with my head. But I definitely think that rushing into anything right now would be a mistake."

I bit my lip and angled myself slightly as I looked at Van's face. "I think we need to get something out of the way. It may make this whole situation a lot easier."

Van smirked. "What's that?"

"I think you should kiss me. If the kissing is terrible, if you feel like you're kissing Charlie, we won't even have to worry about anything else. If the kissing sucks, it won't matter that you're vers or want to suck me or spread your legs for me," I whispered breathily as I repeated his words from earlier.

Van growled. "You're a damn little tease, you know that?"

I licked my lips.

"Are you drunk?" Van narrowed his eyes.

I shook my head. "Nah, just buzzed enough to have no filter. But I'm sober enough to know exactly what I'm doing." I stared at his lips before bringing my eyes to meet his. "And yes, this *is* just a not-so-sneaky way to get a kiss. But it's not a bad idea. Maybe we're all worked up and worried about something between us messing up our little triad when in reality it won't ever go anywhere because you kiss like a dying goldfish."

Van's eyes sparkled with laughter. "Never had any complaints. Maybe it's *you* who kisses like a slobbery dog."

I leaned closer. "Guess it's worth taking me for a test drive. See if all this worry is even worthwhile."

Van's lips brushed against mine and I moaned softly as a jolt of heat and electricity traveled through my body. With a gentle press of his mouth, Van deepened the kiss. I opened my lips slightly and gasped when his hot tongue peeked out to taste me. I darted my tongue to meet his and groaned at how good he tasted. Soft, warm lips and tongues caressed and teased for several moments. At the exact moment when I would have very much liked to crawl onto Van's lap, straddle him, and take things a bit further, we heard a car door slam. Charlie was home.

Breaking apart, both of us breathing heavily, we grinned at each other like loons.

"So," I hedged.

"So," Van repeated.

"No slobbery dogs or dying goldfish."

"Nope."

"Did you feel like you were kissing Charlie?" I asked hesitantly.

"Fuck no. If kissing Charlie was like that, I would have been doing it long ago," Van teased.

I laughed. "I'm sure he'd love to know that. So, the experiment worked. Kissing is great. Now what?" I knew I wanted to drag him to bed, but I also knew that wasn't the smartest thing we could do in our situation.

Van was quiet for a moment. "I have a proposal."

"I'm listening." I heard a faint sound of water turning on in the house and realized we likely had just enough time to talk while Charlie showered and then he'd probably come find us.

"So, Trent already thinks we're together. Which, in reality, makes him about as dumb and gullible as anyone I've ever met. Really? You showed up on our porch last night and we're together today?" Van scoffed.

I shrugged. "He's always been insecure and convinced I was cheating on him. In his mind, I probably hightailed it to whoever I was fucking around with."

"Well, I say we use that to our advantage. Let Trent see us around places. Do you have to be on campus much?" Van asked.

"I have to go a couple days a week, but most of my time is at the school."

"Let's try to work it so I can go with you. I'll walk you to and from where you need to be on campus. That way, Trent thinks we're together. Plus, he can't get violent." Van rubbed the back of his fingers on my thigh. "May make him move on quicker."

"I don't think that's completely necessary, but I won't turn down the chance to get back at him *and* have a hot escort walking me around campus. Is that your proposal?"

"Part of it. The second part involves a favor for me."

I raised my brows.

"So, Charlie and I are part of this small business group here in town. It's local business owners from here and surrounding areas. We meet once a month," Van explained.

"Okaaay," I drawled, not really sure what my part would be.

"Well, there's a lady and her son who own a small car dealership in the neighboring town. She's obnoxious and loud; he's weasely and gives me the creeps—his name is Topher."

I grimaced.

"Yeah, I know." Van pretended to shiver. "They are both bound and determined that Topher and I go out on a date. So far, I've been able to dodge—and in reality, I have no issues just saying *not interested*—but having you attend the upcoming gathering as my date would be great. One, I could maybe convince Topher and Mommy dearest that I'm not available. Two, I could spend the evening with you. Definite bonus." Van winked.

"What kind of event? Just like a meeting?" I wrinkled my nose.

"No, we meet once a month, but twice a year we have a catered dinner. Most of the business owners donate something or bring samples. It's not *fancy* but it's more than just the monthly meetings."

"How dressy are we talking? I have school clothes, but I spend a lot of my days on the floor with my kids so I dress nice but comfortable," I explained.

"Maybe business casual?"

I frowned. "I don't think my wardrobe is ready for that." God, I hated not having any money to spend.

Van pursed his lips and tapped a finger on them. "How about we go shopping? I bet we could get you an outfit or two and write them off as a business expense—I think Charlie is hoping you'll take part in the business more than just an hour or two at a time once you're able. You'll need the clothing for future events."

I narrowed my eyes. "That feels a lot like pity or charity. I hate that I don't have the money for new clothes right now—and I'd love to be your fake date—but I don't want you buying me clothes." Weird how I'd grown up a lot. Three years ago, when Trent wanted to shower me with gifts, my shallow ass ate that shit up. Now? It was different with Van. I didn't want to look like a greedy loser who took handouts. I was sooo ready to be self-sufficient and have a real job.

"Look, we can ask Charlie, but he let me use the business expense budget for a couple nicer outfits a while back because I was going to be wearing them for events that pertained to the bar. I think it's totally legit and it's definitely not pity or charity." Van leaned close and nuzzled my ear. "What do you say? Tomorrow we go see your parents then next weekend we go shopping?"

My breath hitched and I nodded. "Yeah, sounds good. I'm usually swamped and exhausted on most school nights, so weekend is the best. You don't *have* to go with me." I felt like I *had* to say that, but the idea of going shopping with Van had me buzzing with anticipation.

"Nah, I say we make a day of it. It'll be fun." He winked.

"So, we're just faking a relationship? Just to fend off Topher and get back at Trent?" I really wanted more than that, but I knew we'd pretty much agreed to take it slow.

Van chewed his lip. "I think we use our *fake* relationship to our advantage. If Charlie catches on, we can say it's just a ruse. But we use the time to get you settled in, get to know each other as adults rather than kids, and see where things go."

I quirked a brow. "And if it goes somewhere more than just friends?" I *really* wanted it to go somewhere more, but I also appreciated not rushing into things. I *was* fresh out of a long-term, not-so-healthy relationship.

"We break it to Charlie gently. I think defiantly telling him we're going to give it a go *now* would likely piss him off and make things tense. And really, if we're being honest, it wouldn't make a lot of sense. You show up, we're both attracted and have fond memories of the past, so we decide to date in twenty-four hours?" Van shook his head with a smirk. "No, I think it's better if we ease into it, make sure you and I are both on the same page and agree there's something between us more than just a physical attraction, then letting him know we're together and serious about giving it a shot later may go over better." Van tipped my chin up and kissed me. "But I need you to know that I won't push something with you aside—if we both agree it's what we want—just because Charlie gets his panties in a bunch."

My heart gave a warm squeeze. "What level of taking it slow are we talking here?" I wanted more than kisses.

Van thought for a moment. "Can we just see where things go? I know neither of us would push the issue if the other isn't comfortable, so maybe we just let things happen as they happen. Either way, we build on the friendship and not just on anything sexual."

I nodded. "That sounds good." I bit my lip. "I'm kinda a bit screwed in the head when it comes to love and romance and sex thanks to Trent. I may need your help to work things out."

"What do you mean?" Van asked gently and touched my cheek.

"Trent said a lot of things…" I began.

The patio door slid open and Van dropped his hand. "There you guys are. Whoa, you started without me?" Charlie popped the top on a beer and sat down in a chair near the firepit.

"Not our fault you stayed so long at the bar. You get plans made?" Van asked casually.

Charlie took a long pull on his beer and then nodded as he swallowed. "Yep, I've got it worked out." He glanced my way. "*You* are a genius and I'm excited about this expansion."

I smiled and shrugged. "Can't really take credit for a mistake."

"Nope, this new avenue is all you, Squirt," Charlie teased.

I groaned. "So, what's the plan?"

Van and I turned down more to drink and listened as Charlie filled us in on the plan to introduce coffee, tea, and breakfast items in the mornings and some brunch options to transition into the lunch rush. He was working on details for hiring morning shift employees, locally sourcing coffee, tea, breakfast, and brunch items, and hyping up the new addition to Byrd and Badger.

"We'll likely slowly add the morning stuff in during the week and then have a big shebang on the weekend as an official *grand opening* of sorts," Charlie explained.

I yawned. The buzzy feeling was quickly turning into a sleepy feeling. "What time are we going to Mom and Dad's?"

"Told them we'd be there around noon. Does that give you enough time to get your school stuff done?" Charlie asked.

"Yeah, that works." I stood and gathered up the empty cans while Van grabbed the two mugs.

"You need me at the bar tomorrow?" Van asked.

"Nah, we've got all the shifts covered. Figured you'd come to lunch with us. Kendall has to work, but I told Mom her three favorite boys would be there." Charlie finished his beer. "Well, if you two are tapping out so early, I guess I'll head in too."

"It's not that early. You got started late," I told my brother as I walked into the house and tossed the cans in the recycling bin.

"Semantics," Charlie teased.

"Hey, if Sky were to come with us to the local business owners event and needed some dressier clothes than his Kindergarten duds, would we be able to use the expense account for that?" Van asked Charlie.

Charlie paused for a moment. "Yeah, that's what it's there for. Sky, you *want* to come to that?"

I shrugged. "It's not like I've got a lot of other social events taking place. I wouldn't mind as long as it's okay with you."

"Definitely. Can get a little boring at times, but we'd love to have you there as a face of Byrd and Badger. Just let me know when you want to go shopping." Charlie tossed his beer can in the bin.

"Gonna take him next weekend. Just tell me what I need to do to turn it in on expenses," Van stated in a way that clearly said he wasn't open to arguing about it.

Charlie glanced back and forth between the two of us and my face flushed with nerves. Was he already onto us? Was he pissed? But my brother just shrugged. "Yeah, sure. Just let me know the total and I'll reimburse you."

Charlie headed to his room. "G'night," he called.

Van followed me down the other hallway and stopped next to my doorway. "Can I come in for just a minute? Just in case he walks back through."

I nodded and opened the door to my room. The second the door closed, Van wrapped me in his arms and held me tight.

I melted into him and buried my face in his chest.

"It's really good to have you home, Sky," Van murmured against my head.

"Good to be here. Didn't realize how much I needed this —all of it."

Van held me for a few more moments before tipping my chin and kissing me gently. "Sleep tight." He glanced around the room. "We should talk to Charlie about making this more of a bedroom for you rather than a futon in an office."

I smiled and shrugged. "It's not that big of a deal." My stupid heart flip-flopped as I thought about the possibility of spending nights in *Van's* bed. No, we were taking it slowly. That was for the best. Right? "Goodnight," I whispered.

SIX

VAN

THE THREE OF us ended up at the Byrd family home at exactly noon the next day. Sky had been adorably anxious as he flitted around getting his school work done—I had this weird desire and hope that I'd sometime be able to help him with cutting out colored shapes and making number and letter cards for his *Kindergarten babies* as he called them—and he was doubly adorable as we walked toward the backdoor of his childhood home.

"Oh my God," he croaked, "this is so damn surreal. I'd told myself this place was a *never again*, that these people considered me dead to them, and now I'm walking in like nothing has changed."

I wanted to pull him close and kiss the top of his head. Instead, I let Charlie lead the way up the stairs and I brushed my hand against Sky's.

He took my fingers in his for the briefest moment.

"It's all good," I whispered. "Neither Charlie or I would let you walk into something harmful." I gave his hand a quick squeeze before we followed Charlie through the door.

Sky smiled gratefully and then his eyes went wide as his mother appeared in the doorway with his father close behind.

"Your eye," Robin gasped.

"It's fine," Sky said quickly as he stepped closer.

"It's not fine and we will discuss it," she spoke sternly, "but later." She gave a watery smile. "I knew you were talented, intelligent, and destined to be something so very special," Robin's eyes glistened as she looked Sky up and down—it was a running joke that she must have really loved Stephen to marry him and change her name to Robin Byrd, and she brought her youngest along on the ride by naming him Sky, "but I never knew just how damn tenacious you were." Robin reached out and yanked Skyler into her arms and sobbed into his chest.

When they finally broke apart, Stephen pulled his son into a welcoming hug.

I couldn't help the sting in my eyes and the smile on my face. It was like watching my own family—the Byrds *were* my true family from the moment my grandma died, and maybe even before. Grandma always said she had no worries leaving this earth because she knew the Byrds would care for me as much as she did.

Sky wiped at his eyes as we made our way into the kitchen. "I like this talented, intelligent, and special stuff, but tenacious?"

Robin's eyes went wide as she sniffled. "You're kidding, right? The three of us texted you *weekly*. Religiously. I don't know, maybe Charlie missed a week here and there."

Charlie shook his head and I knew he was telling the truth. He had three years of texts on his phone. Wouldn't even upgrade his phone because he didn't want to lose the weekly texts he'd sent to Sky, even when there was *never* a reply.

"Guess you can get that upgrade now," I mumbled to

Charlie as we took in the heartwarming, somewhat bittersweet reunion.

He snorted.

"I know your dad and I didn't miss a single week—sometimes I texted more than once a week. I called weekly for a while and then monthly. I kept thinking I'd wear you down." A tear trickled down her cheek and she swiped at it before pulling Sky into another hug.

He looked at me and Charlie, questioning and desperate, over her shoulder. "I didn't know." He pulled back, his hands on her shoulders. "Mom, I swear I didn't know. Trent got me a new phone the next day. New plan, new number, blank contacts." He looked as if he was about to lose it. "I'm so sorry. I didn't know."

"Would you have finally answered? Ever believed we weren't the enemy?" Robin whispered, her hands on her son's cheeks.

Sky's face fell and he shook his head. "I honestly don't know. Until this," he gestured toward his eye, "I was convinced I was stuck with no way out. For a while, I truly believed you guys were the problem. Even once I admitted to myself that I'd opted to throw you all under the bus for Trent, I assumed I'd ruined any chance of fixing things."

Stephen placed a hand on Sky's shoulder and Robin shook her head. "Never. You can *never* ruin anything with us. We're your family. We love you. We might have disagreements and differing opinions, but we will *never* not love you."

Sky frowned. "Differing opinions? You know I'm gay? I can't change that. That's how this all started."

Robin smiled and huffed gently. "I think we've known longer than you. Maybe? Either way, we are one hundred percent okay with it. All we've ever wanted for our boys was for you to both be safe, happy, and healthy." She gave a worried scowl. "Are you upset we didn't let you know our suspicions?"

Sky shook his head. "No, not really. It would have maybe helped, but knowing my dramatic, stubborn ass, I may have flipped out over that as well. I'm still dramatic and stubborn..."

"And we wouldn't have you any other way," Robin interrupted.

Sky smiled and continued, "But I've grown up a lot and teaching has helped in a lot of ways. I may still be dramatic and stubborn, but I'm maybe a little more mature and better at handling emotions?" He smiled, albeit a bit sadly. "The main thing I want to focus on is leaving the past in the past and moving on with people who truly respect, support, and love me."

"Excellent," Charlie interjected. "We love you. We're glad you're back home. Please tell Mom not to kill me for keeping you from them for *less than* forty-eight hours. Now, can we please eat? I'm starving. All this fawning over the squirt here is giving me an inferiority complex," he teased.

We all laughed. Robin smacked Charlie in the back of the head. Charlie put Sky in a headlock. And we settled on the patio to eat Chinese carryout Stephen had picked up right before we arrived.

"If you think I'm spending a single moment of your first day back home cooking or cleaning up dishes, you're severely mistaken." Robin handed out Styrofoam plates and we all loaded up on noodles, chicken, beef, veggies, egg rolls, crab Rangoon, and rice.

We ate quietly for a few moments before Stephen cleared his throat. "Did you bring your stuff today?"

"Stuff?" Sky asked with an egg roll halfway to his mouth.

"Your furniture and everything is still upstairs. But you can bring your clothing and such whenever if you didn't bring it today," Robin explained before taking a bite of rice and chicken.

Shit.

Sky's eyes went wide and Charlie cleared his throat.

"Oh, um," Sky stammered. "Um, I was planning to stay with Charlie and Van."

Robin and Stephen glanced at each other.

"Oh," Robin said. She looked devastated. "We've kept your room for you all this time."

Sky winced. "I'm sorry. I don't want to make you feel bad, but living with my brother is bad enough…"

"Hey," Charlie squawked.

"I'm supposed to be a grown-up and on my own. Moving back to live with my parents—unless one of you is ill or something?—is not the direction I want to be headed," Sky said softly.

Robin and Stephen cracked up laughing.

"We're kidding. I changed your room into a little gym about a year ago. You're out of luck," Robin crowed. "If you *need* a place, you're welcome to the guest room. But you'll have to switch to the couch when Aunt Jean comes to visit."

Sky rolled his eyes and tossed a fortune cookie at Robin's head. "That was mean. I was freaking out thinking you were crushed."

"Charlie bought that house specifically because it had a room for you if and when you ever came home," Stephen said. "We knew there was no way you'd opt for us over your brother and Van."

Sky smiled. "I mean, I'd prefer to be on my own or at least be able to contribute, but I really appreciate Charlie being there for me."

"You'll do as much as you can," Charlie said.

"Maybe you cook? Clean? Help in that way?" Robin suggested.

Sky thought for a moment and nodded. "Yeah, actually that would be good. My school hours allow me to be home by about four. I could do dinner and straighten up the house. Depending on what hours you guys work?" He glanced toward me and Charlie.

"We'll work it out. Sometimes we're at work together, sometimes we take opposite shifts." Charlie nudged Sky. "This semester isn't forever. This time next year, or even earlier, you'll have a full-time teaching job."

"There's no guarantee of that," Sky began.

"Then you'll work full-time for us," I interjected. "You don't need to worry about it for now."

Sky took a deep breath like he wanted to argue—I knew he wanted to argue, he hated being reliant on us—but he blew it out slowly and nodded. "I hate it, but I appreciate it."

"Just pay it forward sometime," Charlie said around a bite of noodles.

"Yeah, like when Charlie is old and in diapers, you can take care of him," I teased.

The whole group laughed and we continued eating.

The entire afternoon was spent laughing, telling stories, catching up, and just enjoying each other's company before it was time to leave.

"I wish Kendall could be here," Robin lamented.

"She and I will come over next weekend. She's off," Charlie offered as we headed toward the door to go home.

"Van and Sky?" Robin asked.

"We'll see how much school work I have," Sky started. "And I have to go shopping with Van for dressier clothes."

Robin raised a brow and glanced between the two of us.

I fought a blush. Robin knew me. She knew Sky. Did she notice something between us? Hell, was there even *something* between us?

"We're outfitting him for the local business events. He's

not full-time at Byrd and Badger, but we want him in front of the community. Especially since he's the brains behind the new addition," Charlie mentioned the coffee and tea idea he'd told his parents about earlier. He gave his parents a hug and bounded down the steps.

Sky hugged his parents, clinging longer than Charlie had, promised to visit often, and stepped out the door.

I gave Stephen a pat on the back and hugged Robin. "Guess they aren't waiting on me," I joked as I turned to leave.

"Van?" Robin called out quietly.

I turned to look at her, my brows raised.

"Take care of him," she whispered. "You two are good for each other."

I started to argue, but instead just pressed my lips together and smiled softly with a nod. "I will." My heart warmed to know that Sky and I—if and when we decided what we had was worth taking to the next step—at least had Robin's blessing.

THE NEXT SATURDAY, Sky climbed into my car and we headed out for our shopping excursion. I purposely made sure he had finished all of his school work for the day so he wouldn't have any excuses to head home early. I planned to spend the entire day with him.

As I pulled onto the interstate toward the next closest shopping area, Sky glanced my way with a frown.

"Um, are we going to Northwood? Isn't the mall down here easier?" he asked.

"Just thought it would be nice to get out of town," I answered with a shrug, although I felt guilty. Maybe my plan was going to backfire.

Sky was quiet for a moment. He shifted in his seat and fidgeted before blowing out a breath. "Look, this is a new start for me and I don't want to seem ungrateful or anything —but I've got to make a point not to get lost again. Trent never wanted to go out in public with me. If we went out, we acted like buddies. I'm not one for huge displays of public affection, but if being seen in public with me is going to be an issue for you, we maybe need to rethink some things." He lifted his chin as if to punctuate the words.

I pulled off at the exit and parked in a Starbucks parking lot. Leaning over, I took his cute jutted chin between my thumb and finger, kissed his chin, and then brushed my lips over his. "Being seen in public with you isn't a problem for me." I nuzzled my nose against his. "I should have just said something and communicated with you. Staying in town means we run the risk of seeing Charlie's or Kendall's friends, people I work with, maybe people you work with, people your parents know."

"That sounds very much like you're worried about being seen in public with me," Sky murmured against my lips.

"I was thinking we could kinda make this a date. Maybe a hand holding here and there? A little kiss? My arm around you in a way that may not look like a buddy? If we're taking things slow and not throwing ourselves at Charlie, it may be easier to just be us if we don't have *as* many eyes around us." I snaked my hand behind his head and pulled him close before capturing his mouth with mine. Sky whimpered and melted into the kiss, his tongue darting out to taste mine.

When we broke apart, Sky's face was flushed and he smiled. "Okay, I can see the thinking. But two things," he said.

I raised a brow and waited.

"First, let's talk about these things in the future. I'm coming from a situation where *zero* decisions were mine to make—or if I got to make a decision, it was wrong or I spent weeks being ridiculed—so I'm kinda defensive." Skyler scowled. "It's like I'm stuck between believing that I don't deserve to make decisions or I suck at it and being determined to start standing up for myself and being a part of the decisions made." He leaned close and trailed kisses along my jaw. "So, when it felt like you were making a decision without including me, I got anxious and defensive."

I kissed him and pressed my forehead against his. "I get that. Completely. And I'm sorry for not just talking to you."

We sat quietly for a moment.

"And two?" I asked.

"Huh?"

"You said there were two things," I mumbled against his lips.

"Oh, right." Sky smiled. "Buy me a chai latte?" He pointed toward the Starbucks drive-thru.

I laughed and pulled into the line.

A couple minutes later, armed with our chai lattes, I pointed the car toward Northwood and we settled in for a comfortable fifteen minutes of chit-chat and tasty drinks.

"We definitely need a *good* chai latte at Byrd and Badger," Sky mused as he took a sip. "Not all chai lattes are created equal."

I took his hand and squeezed it. *How had I gone from sleeping around and not wanting to settle down to holding hands with a guy I'd known from birth and thinking about a future? And how did it feel so right and perfect?* "Well, I say we put you in charge of being a taste-tester. I think Charlie has about six lined up to try, so you will definitely need to be in on that. I like the drink, but I'm more into coffee."

"I like tea better than coffee, so I'll volunteer to make sure we've got the best tea around," Sky offered.

"Can I just say that I love that you're talking about the

business as if it's yours? I know it's not your dream, but having you be part of it with us is something Charlie and I always wanted." I kept his hand in mine as we pulled into the mall and found a parking spot. "So, I'm thinking we do our shopping for clothes first then lunch. Then we can hit some of the other stores as just-for-fun shopping, just look around. Maybe hit a movie? Light dinner before we go home?" I'd never been so nervous suggesting date ideas.

Sky's face fell. "That all sounds great, but I maybe have enough money for a light lunch. Nothing more."

I shifted over the console and once again pulled his face close to mine. "Sky, I've missed you. I missed your dramatic, punk-ass when I left at eighteen. I've missed you since coming home and finding out you weren't around. Getting you back in my life means a lot. At first, it was because I had a friend back—I know you were always relegated to little brother status back then—but the moment I saw you on our porch, I knew I wanted to grow that history, that friendship, as adults. But then that flicker of attraction took hold and I realized I want more than friendship." I kissed him, slow and soft. "I'm one hundred percent on board with getting to know each other, taking things slowly, treading gently around the Charlie issue."

"But?" Sky frowned.

"But I'd *really* like to take you on a date. Not charity or pity, just me treating a man I like to a meal and movie. Please?" My voice was husky and desperate and I didn't even care. I wanted this with him—it was such an insignificant thing, but I wanted it to happen.

Sky stared at me for a moment as if trying to decide. "Let me buy lunch—we have to go somewhere cheap—and you can treat the movie and dinner." He dipped his head, but not before I caught the flush of his cheeks.

I pulled him close and kissed him, hard and fast. "Thank

you. I don't know why it feels like such a big thing when it's really not, but thank you."

We drained the rest of our chai lattes and climbed from the car. I adjusted a backpack on my back.

"You thinking this is going to turn into quite the trek or something?" Sky teased.

I shook my head. "No, I just prefer to be able to stick things in the bag. Backpack or crossbody messenger type bag is perfect to toss little purchases in. Plus, it holds my wallet and keys along with medication in case I start getting a headache. Throw in a bottle of water and some band-aids and I'm a regular walking-first-aid station."

"You're kinda great, you know that? I do the same when I go on fieldtrips. My first year in education, a couple guys— who are no longer in the program—gave me a bunch of shit for toting around a bag on a field trip. I bitched about it to Trent; he laughed at me and said I was bringing it on myself being a pussy who needed to carry a bag." Sky's words brought a stormy look over his face, but he shook it off. "I think the bag carrying men of the world are clearly a superior species."

"Totally agree. I mean, we'll see who's a pussy when you and I are prepared for anything with our bags-o'-plenty and the Trents of the world are left with uncovered hangnails and headaches because they have no band-aids or ibuprofen in their pants pocket." I nodded sagely and we both laughed. "Do you have a game plan for tackling this shopping trip?"

"First stop, bathroom. Then we can hit the clothing stores." Sky bumped his hip against mine. "As much as I hate the thought of not being able to pay for my own clothes, I have to say that I adore shopping and I'm kinda excited."

I snaked my hand around his waist and pulled him into a brief side hug before we walked through the mall entrance.

After the bathroom, I convinced Sky I couldn't shop

without a fountain drink, chocolate covered peanuts, and gummy worms from the candy shop next to the food court.

He rolled his eyes. "You were always just a big goofy kid," he said as we waited in line to pay for the items.

"Don't act like you won't be grateful for the sustenance when you're on your fifteenth pair of pants," I teased.

"Is that like a gallon of Coke?" Sky gestured to the *very* large Styrofoam cup in my hand.

"Figured we'd split it." I shrugged and paid for my purchase. "Okay, where to first?" I tossed the bags of candy into my backpack.

"Where did you get your clothes for events?" Sky asked as we stood in the middle of the mall and glanced down the three extending corridors.

"Well, I planned to just go to Kohls or something, but Charlie insisted I go somewhere a bit higher-end." I rolled my eyes. "I ended up finding everything at Jefferson's. They offer free tailoring with your purchase."

"Is it super expensive?" Sky worried his bottom lip. "Maybe I should try one of the cheaper stores?"

I shook my head. "Nope, Charlie already told me that I had to steer you toward the nicer places. Jefferson's isn't terribly expensive. I mean, more than what you'd pay for an outfit other places, but it's good quality and they'll make sure it fits you perfectly. In the long run, it's better quality for your money."

"Did Charlie make you practice that speech?" Sky narrowed his eyes.

My cheeks heated. "He may have suggested I have a rebuttal prepared."

Sky huffed and shook his head. "You two haven't changed at all." He waved a hand toward the wing of the mall that displayed the Jefferson's sign. "Lead on."

SEVEN

SKY

I WAS CLEARLY IN A DREAM. But in all honesty, I didn't want to wake up. One thing I *had* to stop doing was comparing everything Van said and did to Trent. But after three years of Trent putting me down, laughing at me, never taking time for me, blah, blah, blah, it was very hard to not put Van on a pedestal and worship at his feet.

Van was *not* perfect. I knew that. In theory. And I most definitely didn't want to be starry-eyed and gaga over him simply because he was *better than Trent*. Let's face it, it wouldn't take much to be better than Trent. I'd known Van for sixteen years, and now I had the chance to get to know the grown-up version. I knew Van was so very *good*. And I wanted to like him, explore whatever this attraction with him was, and see if things felt right to move forward *because of Van*, not because he was just so much better than Trent.

I walked next to my gentle giant. He had a backpack on in a shopping mall and didn't even bat an eye. I seriously thought he could have carried a purse with no issues and wouldn't have thought a thing about it. He slurped his Coke and smiled as he offered me a drink.

I rolled my eyes but begrudgingly took a sip and refused to admit I was glad he'd brought the drink along.

In the time since we'd walked into the mall, Van had touched me more than Trent touched me in public during our entire three years. Van and I weren't making out in the mall—I definitely wasn't into that—but the small touches here and there, his hand brushing across the small of my back, and the way he stood close and spoke quietly in my ear were all indicators that Van wasn't ashamed to be seen next to me. It made me want to say *fuck it* to taking our time and treading lightly around Charlie.

Trent always said he had a reputation to live up to among his friends and that meant being a *man's man* and not dating twinks. When we were alone, he'd accuse me of luring him in with my silk panties, make-up, and lack of a gag reflex. He'd tell me he was so weak for falling for me. But all of those things that he supposedly fell for were also things he despised and refused to admit—in public—that he found attractive. Trent had *a lot* of issues and I mistakenly thought I could fix them.

We walked through the door of Jefferson's and I immediately loved it. It was a mall storefront, but it didn't have the huge open front. There was a single door and once inside it was as if you were in a free-standing store rather than a mall store.

"Welcome to Jefferson's, gentlemen," a gorgeous man with silver-blond hair and piercing blue eyes greeted us. "I'm Jared and I'll be happy to assist you in *any* way you need today."

I smiled politely, but inside I was laughing.

Van stepped closer to me and touched the small of my back. "My boyfriend is looking for some business casual looks for a few upcoming business events."

Jared smirked as he glanced between us. "Excellent. My day just took a turn for the better."

I swear Van vibrated next to me. "Would it be possible for us to look on our own and holler at you if we need help?" he nearly growled his request.

Jared pursed his lips. "Well, that's a lot less fun, but sure." He glanced toward the door where a man sauntered in with a smile. "Perfect," Jared purred. "I'll be busy with Cian, but you boys just yell if you need something." He made a beeline for the new customer.

"Is it weird that he seemed to be offering to fuck either or both of us in the dressing room?" I whispered. "Seems like an establishment like this would frown upon that." The idea of a threesome in the dressing room was kinda exciting—but I knew my *I'm-a-teacher-I-can't-get-caught-fucking-in-the fitting-room* self would never allow for it.

Although...

A threesome behind closed doors? Pretty sure my *I'm-a-teacher-but-that-doesn't-mean-I-can't-get-kinky* self would totally approve.

Hmmm...a very interesting thought indeed. I'd brought up the idea of playing around and having a threesome to Trent once. He'd flipped out, called me a slut, and said if he wasn't keeping my greedy little ass satisfied, I could leave. So yeah, Trent was *not* on board with adding a third just for fun. I wondered what Van would think.

"I'm sure he's perfectly professional with the straight guys or the ones he can't read. I kinda like that he immediately knew we were together." Van scowled. "Wasn't thrilled that he basically asked to undress you."

Clearing my head with a quick shake, I chuckled. "Well, I've got someone else in mind for that job anyway."

"Need help with your zipper?" Van teased.

I held a hand to my chest and fake gasped. "Well, I never.

I'll have you know that I'm *not* that type of boy." I batted my lashes. "But if you want to help me find the perfect pants to compliment my purple silk panties, I'd be down."

Van's nostrils flared. "Are you seriously wearing purple silk panties right now?" he whispered gruffly.

I made a *maybe* face and licked my lips.

"I swear to God, Sky. I will lock you in that dressing room and fuck you right here and now," he threatened with a delicious gleam in his eyes.

I snorted. "Damn, now I wish I *was* wearing the purple silk. But alas, they aren't the most practical for mall shopping and trying on clothes. Plain cotton hipster briefs for today's outing." I smirked. "But I could be persuaded to wear something a little sexier the next time we go out." I grimaced. "Not that I expect you to be taking me out all the time or anything."

Van took a deep breath through his nose as if trying to calm himself—not gonna lie, I kinda loved it—and smiled before holding his hand out to me. "One, I love spending time with you. Two, it's best that I not know about underwear choices if I'm expected to be a gentleman."

Is it weird that I'm stuck between wanting Van to either be a gentleman and treat me like a queen or get down and dirty and do his nastiest best?

I shook off the thought. The mall was not the place for that type of thinking.

We wandered toward the fitting rooms as I glanced at the clothing options hanging on racks and folded on shelves.

"Maybe I can give you tiny details about my under garments...a color here, a style there, just to keep you wondering and interested," I teased.

"Interested is *not* an issue," Van growled as he herded me into the dressing room.

I took the stall farthest from the entrance—for privacy

and because it was the largest of the five—and Van dropped his bag and drink onto the bench.

"Um, we kinda skipped the part where we picked out clothes to actually try on." I laughed as I glanced around the empty fitting room and realized we'd been talking underwear the whole time and didn't pick up a single item of clothing.

"Let's do this: I'll bring like ten pairs of pants. Once we get the right pants, we'll move on to shirts," Van suggested. "Oh, what size do you wear?"

I told him my pant and shirt sizes and then frowned. "Why pants first? Is that like some sort of secret shopping tip I've never learned?"

"Once you have the pants, shirts are easier," Van stated this like it was general knowledge.

"Do I get a say in any of these choices?" I elbowed him.

"Of course. If you don't like any of the pants I bring, you can request more or go out there and search for some for yourself."

"And the shirts?" I raised a brow.

"Same thing."

I shrugged and waved him on. "I await your choices."

While Van was gone, I sipped the Coke and ate a few gummy worms. The chocolate covered peanuts smelled yummy, but I didn't want to risk chocolate on the clothes.

"I hope you're ready for this amazingness," Van announced as he walked to my little cubicle, his voice was a mixture of truly happy to be spending time with me and excitement over his fashion choices for me.

I actually *was* intrigued to see what Van had picked for me. He wasn't a slouch when it came to fashion, but I also wouldn't have categorized him as highly fashionable.

He pushed the door open and dropped several pairs of pants onto the bench before hanging the rest of them. "Okay, here's the plan. Try each on, I want to see them even if you hate them—it will help me know what you like and how things fit."

"You sure that's not just a ruse to get to maybe see me naked?" I waggled my brows.

Van scoffed and took the gummy worms and Coke with him to the bench outside of my fitting room.

I started on the folded pants first.

"Eeww," I announced. "Pleats?" I buttoned the first pair but knew immediately that they were going in the *no* pile.

"Let me see," Van demanded.

I opened the door.

"Shirt off. That shirt is fine with jeans, but you can't get the perfect pants when paired with a casual t-shirt."

I narrowed my eyes at Van. "Have you been watching What Not to Wear or Queer Eye?" I pulled the shirt over my head.

Van's eyes lingered on my chest for a moment and my cheeks heated. He pulled his gaze from my torso and studied the pants. Ignoring my question, Van shook his head. "Yeah, those are a no. You've got a gorgeous body," he paused and licked his lips, "but that cut is doing nothing for you. Next."

By the third pair of pants, I'd realized that Van was turned on seeing me in nothing but pants, so I played it up as I modeled each pair and made sure to give him plenty of glimpses of my ass.

Van was a good sport and appeared to be trying very hard to just drink his Coke, eat his gummy worms, and appraise each pair of pants. But the fiery gleam in his eyes told a different story. "You're trouble, you know that?" he asked as he sucked his lip between his teeth before popping another gummy worm.

I threw a saucy glance over my shoulder and wiggled my ass.

Van popped up from the bench and adjusted himself.

I smiled. "I think I like these." I ran a hand over my ass.

"Yeah, those are good," Van muttered and cleared his throat.

I decided on two pairs of pants that fit really well and would go with a lot of shirt options.

Van headed off to gather shirts while I placed the discarded pants on the *return* rack.

The shirts went a lot quicker. And were harder to choose because there were several that I really liked. Van talked me into getting three of them because the store was having a *buy two, get one 50% off.*

Once we'd piled the *to purchase* items to the side, Van stepped into the dressing room and began to help rehang the shirts I wasn't getting. For a moment, I just watched him in the mirrors. My gentle giant, taking care of me, helping me clean up, brightening my day just by being there.

He glanced up and caught me staring. "What?"

"Thank you for today. It's kinda overwhelming, but it's also really nice. Just easy and nice. It's been a long time since I've had that." I stepped closer to him and unbuttoned the last shirt I'd tried on.

Van's eyes watched my every move and his jaw bulged. "You're so damn gorgeous," he whispered.

I removed the shirt and tossed it to the *yes* pile. "Ever had any kind of fun in a dressing room?" I asked, my voice husky. I undid the button on my pants without taking my eyes from Van.

He closed his eyes and breathed deeply. "So much trouble," he whispered.

"That didn't answer my question," I replied.

Van shook his head and stepped closer. Within seconds, his mouth was on mine and his tongue swept in to tangle with mine. The warmth of Van's hands as they trailed down my shoulders, my back, and settled just under the waistband of my pants sent tremors of pleasure through me. With slow, deliberate movements, Van eased the pants over my ass and pushed them down.

I kicked the pants to the side and melted into Van's strong heat.

He continued to devour my mouth, both of us tasting like sugar and desire.

A fully-clothed Van was a stark contrast to me as I stood in only socks and underwear. His hair was lighter and a bit shorter, his skin a more golden color, and everything about him was bigger than me. But as I caught a glimpse of our bodies in the mirror, I thought that nothing had ever looked more perfectly beautiful.

I rocked my hips against his, my dick straining against the cotton material of my underwear. Just as I thought Van was going to back me up and pin me to the wall, he sat on the small bench and pulled me down to straddle his lap.

I laughed and gripped his shoulders to balance myself.

When Van's fingers dug into my hips to hold me steady, the laughter was replaced with a moan. I shifted on his lap, my hard length bumping his abdomen as I wiggled on the bulge under his zipper.

Van's arms snaked up my back and pulled me close, his mouth meeting mine with such gentle strength that I gasped. He took advantage of my open mouth and plunged his tongue in deep. Our wet lips, slick tongues, and warm mouths were almost too much and I whimpered as I rocked on Van's lap. I wanted more, needed to feel his skin against mine, longed for more of his touch.

"God, Sky, I don't know how long I can keep my hands off you." His words were low and gruff before he captured my mouth again.

"We kinda suck at the hands-off thing," I whispered against his lips with a smile.

"Don't talk about sucking right now." Van groaned and pumped his hips up. "I wanna strip you, spread you out, and suck you until you explode for me, and this is *definitely* not the place for that."

A small needy sound escaped from me as I continued to rock my cock against him and rub my ass on his erection. "Charlie would be *very* disappointed to get a call from the mall security office to come pick us up if we got taken in for indecent public behavior," I teased.

Van snorted and shifted so that our swollen dicks got a little breathing room. He pressed his forehead to mine and took a deep breath. "We gotta cool it. I can't go purchase clothing with a hard-on tenting my pants."

"I doubt Jared would care," I teased.

Van grumbled and adjusted himself.

I chuckled. "Carry the clothes in front of you," I suggested.

We sat for several more moments, wrapped in each other's arms, just enjoying the warmth and closeness.

Until Jared called out. "Boys? Everything okay in here? No hanky-panky allowed," he said and then lowered his voice, "unless I'm allowed to be involved."

Van smirked and rolled his eyes. "We're good. Making our final choices."

"Well, that's disappointing," Jared cooed. "I'll see you up front."

I reluctantly stood from Van's lap, my legs still straddled around his.

Van groaned as he stared straight at my bulge. He gripped my hips and pulled me just slightly forward as he pressed his forehead against my stomach. His hot breath brushed over my skin and I shivered. A slight shift downward and his mouth would be on my dick; a drop of precum escaped and I felt it wet my underwear as I moaned.

"Van, this is torture—of the most exquisite kind obviously—but we've gotta stop. I don't want to have to walk in cum-y underwear all day and I'm not letting you buy me *more* clothing." I kissed the top of his head and stepped away.

Van's glazed eyes stared up at me for several beats before he broke from his trance and shook his head. "Shit, sorry. That was intense. Really good, but more than we need to be doing in a dressing room."

"Maybe something we should be doing in more like a bedroom?" I suggested.

He took a deep breath. "God, yes." But then he closed his eyes. "But this doesn't seem like *taking it slow*, you know? And that's what we agreed on." Van turned worried eyes my way.

"We also agreed that we'd let things happen naturally. None of this feels rushed or pushed. We're grown-ups, Van. I *do* get Charlie's concerns, but I'm also not going to withhold something good from myself just because my brother might have a hard time accepting that there's something between us." I pulled my t-shirt over my head.

"If things don't work between us, do you think we can go back to just friends?" Van cocked his head.

"I think we can probably do anything we set our mind to. And if for some reason we can't, Charlie won't lose either of us. He just won't have us at the same time." I shimmied into my jeans and smiled at the slight look of disappointment on Van's face. "I'm not saying we go home and fuck in the kitchen. That's just inviting Charlie to bust in and freak out. But I'm completely okay with this." I gestured toward where we'd been making out on the bench.

Van pulled me into a tight hug and bent just slightly to press a kiss against my temple. "You're kinda amazing, you know that?"

"First I'm trouble and now I'm amazing?" I teased as we gathered our things and headed toward the sales counter.

"Amazing trouble, how's that?" Van bumped my hip.

I pretended to think it over. "It has potential."

Jared gave us a look of *I know what you were doing* and *why didn't you ask me to join* before ringing up the purchase, bagging our items, and wishing us a nice day.

Exiting Jefferson's, I blinked in the brightness of the mall as I reacquainted myself with my surroundings.

"Let's run this out to the car and then we'll grab lunch. Food court?" Van asked.

"I'm on a food court budget," I answered with a smile, "so that's perfect."

We left the mall and my eyes squinted against the glaring sunshine.

"We'll check the movie times, shop around, watch the show, and then grab dinner before we go home, yeah?" Van tossed the bag into the trunk.

"Sounds good," I agreed.

Van took my hand as we walked back toward the mall. "So, lunch?"

We decided on sub sandwiches and carried our food orders to the seating area. As I dug into my food, I watched four young kids play on the little playscape area in the middle of the food court. Without conscious thought, I'd picked a table close to children and that didn't surprise me at all.

"You really like kids, huh?" Van asked with a soft smile.

I nodded. "I really do. It's hard to even explain. Babies are great, and I like ages eight to twelve-ish too, but the four to seven years range is my absolute favorite. I love learning through their eyes, seeing the world as they see it. They're so excited about every single thing and they have so much energy. If we could harness their hearts, energy, intrigue, and unjaded outlook on the world, we could make majorly needed changes."

One of the kids—a little girl with gorgeous black spiral curls and deep brown smiling eyes—stopped by our table and leaned on the dividing fence. Our table was likely only chosen by parents there to watch their children, but I'd instinctively sat there.

"Hi. I'm Jayda. I'm five," the little girl announced as she held up five fingers.

"Hi, Jayda. I'm Skyler. I'm twenty-four," I replied with a smile.

"That's old," she answered with wide eyes. "What's your name?" She looked to Van.

He swallowed his bite of sandwich and looked like a deer in headlights. "Oh, um, I'm Donovan," he stuttered.

"Are you old too?" Jayda asked.

Van chuckled. "Ancient. I'm twenty-six."

Jayda's eyes got even bigger.

A voice called her name and Jayda glanced toward the opposite side of the play area where a lady held a baby on her hip and pointed toward the slide. "That's my momma. I gotta play with my brother. Bye."

I smiled as she ran off. "Cute. See? That's what I mean. Kids that age are just like *Hi, I'm five and we can be forever friends.*"

Van shook his head. "I don't mind kids, but talking to them makes me nervous. It's like I'm afraid I'll say something wrong or scare them or fuck up somehow." He winced. "Like that. Dropping F-bombs in front of kids is usually frowned upon."

"It's weird. I cuss, but I've never had an issue with it at school. It's like my brain just automatically switches to *I'm around little ones, cussing isn't okay* mode." I took a sip of the bottled water I'd purchased with lunch. "My host teacher honestly cusses like a sailor, but I've never heard her slip and she says she's never dropped a single curse word in front of the students in twenty-one years of teaching."

"Impressive." Van popped a chip in his mouth. "So, you want to teach Kindergarten or first grade?"

I nodded. "Definitely. I'll be licensed to teach Kindergarten through sixth, but I'm hoping for a K or first position. Second is about as high as I'd want to go—or at least that's how I feel right now."

A scuffle on the playscape caught my attention, but I continued talking. "The fourth-grade teacher I worked with last semester started out in Kindergarten and swore it was her life-long dream and she'd never leave. But now she says fourth grade is like her calling and she can't imagine doing anything else. So, I'll be open to whatever comes my way."

I scowled at the way a slightly older child was being a bit too rough with Jayda and her brother. The older kid wasn't hurting, but definitely could have been a bit gentler and waited his turn a bit better.

When Jayda ran toward our table with the older boy hot on her heels and a devious grin on his face, I moved slightly to face the play area. Jayda ran past with a shriek—a mixture of *this is fun* and *this isn't cool*—but the boy met my gaze and slowed up. With a bit of an eye roll and a huff, he shrugged his shoulders and changed directions to go play with some kids closer to his own age.

"Oh my God, did you just teacher look him into acting right?" Van whispered.

"What? No? I don't think so," I said with a laugh.

"No, you totally did. He was being an ass, you gave him a look, and he stopped. You totally already have the teacher look down pat. That's kinda amazing." Van took the last bite of his sandwich and wiped his mouth.

I shrugged. "It wasn't a conscious effort. Maybe it's just a natural thing. He probably would have stopped if you'd looked at him too."

Van shook his head. "Nope. You totally had a certain look whether you realized it or not."

I wrinkled my nose. "Great. Let's hope he's not the type of kid to run to his mom who will then come lay me out for interfering with her kid. Despite the fact that she's probably got her nose buried in her phone while Junior wreaks havoc on the playground. And heaven forbid she sees I'm on a date." I held up my hand. "Don't get me wrong, not all parents are like that. I've just seen a few these last couple months who have totally fed into the stereotype of disinterested and/or defensive parents if their kid gets called out on anything." I took a drink. "And you know how you said my look got him to *act right*? I've learned recently that acting *right* is very different for different kids. My idea of *right* may be in vast contrast to another adult's viewpoint. Our kids do what they are taught. And it's not all bad. *Right* is subjective."

Van nodded. "Hadn't thought about that, but I can see it."

I shrugged. "Sorry, I can talk education and behavior and whatnot for days."

"It's fine. I love listening to you talk about something you have such a passion for." Van sipped his water. "So," he started but then paused, "do you want kids? In the future I mean. Is that a part of your dream?"

I swallowed my last bit of turkey and cheese as I thought about the question. "I'm not against having kids one day. Years from now. But I honestly won't be crushed to *not* have my own. I'll have twenty to twenty-five of *my* kids each and every year. It's so weird how quickly I come to think of the students as *mine*. I kinda think that having the heart and energy and time to pour into my students will be for the best. If a child or children of my own comes into the picture, I'm not *against* it. But I feel like my classroom will give me all of the child-centered interaction I could ever want. The idea of going home to just be an adult with my partner is really appealing." I lifted a shoulder. "Again, all subject to change, but that's how I feel for now. You?"

Van cocked his head. "Children wouldn't be a deal breaker for me. But I'm not dreaming of babies and diapers and puke and all of that responsibility." He reached across the table and took my hand. "I'd be happy with a classroom full of your kids." He winked.

My heart nearly fluttered from my chest and I smiled as I squeezed his hand. "Such a sweet talker." I was teasing to keep the mood light, but Trent had *hated* when I talked school or called the students *my kids*. He was always ranting and raving about how there was no way he was working his ass off at a job he hated just so I could buy anything for *those little brats* or stock my classroom supplies. He'd refused to help me pay for a professional development workshop earlier in the year, deeming it *a waste of time and money*. So, having Van listen to me go on and on and seem to immediately *get* that my students were *my kids* was a breath of fresh air and made me love him all the more.

I froze.

Love?

I ran that through my head. Did I love Van? Of course, I did. I'd loved him in some capacity or another since I was a very young child. The love I had for him at the moment was a heady combination of history, friendship, romance, and sexual desire. But even if the romance and sexual desire were removed, I'd still love Van as a friend—as part of my past *and* my future. Even if the rest of it didn't work out.

But please let the rest of it work out. Or at least give it a chance to work out. Let us be able to see if it can go anywhere.

"You wanna check out the movie times?" Van asked as he

studied me. The look on his face told me he wondered where I'd gone in my head.

I nodded with a smile. "Yep. And I want to go to the bookstore, the candle place, and that craft store with all the paper and markers."

"Perfect. Let's go."

We threw our trash away and made our way to the top floor to check what movies were playing.

The suspense movie we opted for didn't start for two hours, so Van bought our tickets and we went to browse some stores. Despite my protests, Van watched me like a hawk and bought items in each store if he thought I liked them. He ended up with a lilac candle, a professional development book, a notebook, a ream of colorful paper, and two packs of markers loaded in his backpack by the end of my browsing. He also purchased himself a book about coffee and tea—he wanted to learn tips on how to brew the best cup —and a candle that smelled like fresh-cut grass.

By the time we were done shopping, we were pushing our movie time, so Van ran the items to the car and gave me his card to go get popcorn and a drink for the movie.

As I stood in line thinking about the fact that I wasn't even *hungry*, but the popcorn smelled so good, a voice from behind startled me.

"Guess you wish you'd stayed put, huh? Now you're going to movies by yourself. Pathetic," Trent sneered.

I turned to glance at him and rolled my eyes as I stepped forward and placed my order. "Not by myself, but thanks for your concern."

"I'm not by myself either," Trent bit out as if irritated that I hadn't asked. "Did you think I'd be mourning your loss?"

Steeling myself to simply blink in acknowledgement of his words and *not* give him ammunition, I pocketed Van's card and took the popcorn and drink from the employee with a thank you. "Well, that's good. Enjoy your day."

I moved to the area where Van would be arriving—hopefully any minute—and stood so I could watch Trent.

Fuck.

Of course, he wasn't done. Trent tucked his popcorn under an arm, sipped his drink, and headed my way.

"Not by yourself, huh?" he asked as he glanced around with an evil smirk.

I stood tall and prepared to ignore and defend if needed.

"Hey, babe." Van appeared like my knight in shining armor. He wrapped an arm around my waist and kissed the side of my head. "You ready?"

Trent gave a look of disdain and walked away.

I sighed. "Thanks for that. He deemed it necessary to speak to me in the concession line *and* follow me over here to continue the digs."

"Such a douche," Van growled and took the drink from my hand before opening the theater door for me.

As we moved off to the side and scanned the area for open seats, I caught a glimpse of Trent walking up the closest set of steps. "Ugh, let's go toward the far wall," I muttered. "Why does he even have to be here?"

Van glanced toward where I'd been looking. Trent sat next to a man, but I couldn't see very well in the dim lighting. "We can leave, pick a different movie?"

I scowled. "Fuck that. No way I'm letting him dictate what movie I watch." I stalked toward the far side and took a seat so that the wall was on my left and Van would be on my right. "I'm going to the restroom before the previews start," I mumbled and shot back out of my chair.

Four minutes later, as I washed my hands at the sink in the mostly empty restroom, a guy walked up and stood right beside me at the neighboring sink.

"You're Skyler, right?" he purred.

I jerked my head to look at him and raised my brows. "Um, yeah?"

"I'm Dayton." He smiled, but it wasn't super friendly. It was more like those scenes in movies where the super popular girls are nice to the lonely girl only to end up doing something terrible.

I nodded. "Okay?"

"I guess I should be thanking you for your little dramatic episode," Dayton continued with a smug smirk.

"I have no idea what you're talking about," I huffed as I dried my hands.

"Well, when you skipped out on Trent, he called me to move in." Dayton shrugged. "We'd been seeing each other off and on for about two years, but with you out of the picture, the space was open for me."

I saw red. My heart leapt to my throat. Swallowing down the irritation, hurt, and anger, I glanced around to be sure I wasn't making a scene. "You've been seeing Trent for nearly two years—knowing he was involved with me—and you're okay with being his second choice when I finally wised up and dumped his ass?"

Dayton licked his lips and gave me a salacious grin. "Sweetie, I was his first call every single time you wouldn't put out—or didn't satisfy him when you did. Don't think I was sitting around lonely and celibate just waiting on Trent to call. But when he did call, I made sure to give him exactly what he was missing with you." He cocked a hip and propped a fist on it. "With you gone, Trent opted to move me in. So, thanks for that."

I narrowed my eyes. "You realize you look almost exactly like me—with the exception of the terrible dye job—and he *never* wants to be seen in public with sissy, girly, twinks." My stomach clenched a little; Trent was at the movies with

Dayton. Maybe Trent only had a problem being seen in public with me.

"Strange," Dayton drawled, "we've been out to eat, to the movies, a couple bar nights. Seems maybe his past issue was with you."

I pursed my lips. "Is he making you pay rent?"

Dayton's eyes flashed. "Well, duh. I'm not some mooch looking for a sugar daddy. I have no problem pulling my weight."

I laughed without humor. "Yeah, well, good luck with that. Talk to me when you realize you're just a rent payment. Talk to me when he separates you from your family, controls your every move, belittles your very existence, and punches you in the face." I turned to leave.

"Trent *is* my family now. I'm sorry all of those things happened to you, but he's a perfect gentleman with me, so maybe you should think about what *you* did to deserve all of that," Dayton called out.

"Started that way with me, too. Wise up," I shot back.

My body shook and my breaths were uneven as I walked back into the movie theater and took my place beside Van.

He took one look at me, put his arm around my shoulders, pulled me close, and whispered, "You okay? Something wrong?"

The lights dimmed and the surround sound boomed through the room.

"I'm fine. I'll tell you later. Ran into Trent's boyfriend—who he's been seeing for two years—in the bathroom," I gritted out and nestled against Van's side.

"What the fuck?" Van growled.

"Let's just watch the movie," I said.

Van tensed as if he wanted to argue, but he let out a slow breath and held me tight as we settled in to the watch the film.

EIGHT

VAN

THE MOVIE ENDED and we stood as the lights slowly came back on.

I purposely dawdled as we waited our turn to leave the row until I'd seen Trent and his date walk down the stairs and around the corner toward the exit.

Once we were away from the crowd and heading toward the parking lot, I took Skyler's hand and gave it a squeeze. "Still want dinner?"

He glanced up at me as if breaking from thought. "Huh? Oh, um," he paused. "Could we get carry-out and just go home?"

My heart did a funny little flip-flop hearing Sky refer to the house as home. *It doesn't mean anything; it's the house he lives in with his brother. Of course, he'd call it his home.* "Sure thing. What do you want?"

Sky pursed his lips for a moment. "Sushi?"

"Sounds good. Can you look up a location while I drive?" I opened his door for him and then got in and started the car.

"Oh my God, this is perfect," Sky said with excitement as he scrolled his phone. "There's this little *What's Good in*

Northwood article and it says the best sushi is located on Heavenly Row." He glanced around and pointed toward one of the exits. "Head out that way. It's downtown a bit more."

I pointed the car toward downtown.

Despite being full of feels from his run-in with both Trent and the boyfriend—at least I *assumed* he was—Sky chuckled as he read the article. "It's called Heavenly Row and three friends went in together to buy three buildings on the downtown square during the city's recent beautification and revitalization project. There's a sushi place—with authentic, top-quality options—a cupcakery, *and* a winery."

"Whoa, Heavenly Row is accurate. You're telling me we can get sushi, cupcakes, and wine all in basically one location? That's brilliant." I slowed to a stop at the stoplight.

"Yeah, says here that the three friends were business majors. Between their own talents and the skills of the families they married into, they ended up with the perfect trio of items to make and sell. So, there's *Stick and Roll*, the sushi shop. *Babycakes*, the cupcake and mini-cakes bakery. And *Vino Valentino*, the winery. All three places make every item they sell fresh and on-site, plus they use locally sourced ingredients and products. The seafood for the sushi arrives daily—which may not be ocean-to-table fresh like on the coast, but for this area, that's damn fresh." Sky did a little dance in his seat. "The three businesses have been open for less than a year—which is probably why I'd never heard of Heavenly Row—but they all seem to be thriving according to the article."

"Well, sushi, cupcakes, and wine sound like the perfect dinner." I drove onto the old courthouse square and found a spot to park in front of *Stick and Roll*.

Once we had our sushi samplers to take home, we went to *Babycakes*. Sky picked out a dark chocolate and salted caramel cupcake. I chose a vanilla bean cupcake with vanilla bean icing piled high. We put the sushi and cupcakes in a little cooler I kept in the trunk and then headed to *Vino Valentino*. After a free tasting of six wines, Sky opted for a blackberry and I picked the rhubarb. Armed with our two bottles, we headed to the car.

"Those places are amazing and I want to come here again. Maybe eat-in sushi, and then take our cupcakes to the winery for dessert and drinks?" Sky smiled broadly and fastened his seatbelt. "Bring Charlie and Kendall, make a night of it."

"That would be fun. I'm sure Charlie would be down. He'll be impressed with the story of the three businesses." I backed out of the parking place and headed toward home. "You want to talk about whatever happened back there at the theater?" I'd seethed through the entire movie and had wanted to march up to Trent's seat and pound his face.

Skyler sobered. "Ugh, not now. Later. Maybe once I've had some wine." He turned in his seat. "Thanks for today. It was one of the best days outside of school that I've had in a long time."

I smiled and took his hand. "You're welcome. Thanks for coming with me. Outside of school, huh? What does a guy have to do to outrank a bunch of Kindergarteners?" I teased.

Sky pretended to ponder the question. "Well, you'd need to be five, beyond excited about learning, tell adorable and funny stories, and think I'm the best thing ever."

"Well, I do love to learn. I think I'm pretty funny. Can't help you on the age part." I shrugged. "And I think you're pretty amazing."

Skyler's eyes flashed as if he were touched by the words. "You're pretty amazing too."

We spent the rest of the short drive talking about some of Sky's favorite students and what he was teaching for the upcoming week. He was already sending out resumes to surrounding school districts—although he hoped to land a job at his host school—and would be graduating in a few short months.

Later, after we'd eaten the most delicious sushi I'd ever tasted, we each ate a quarter of our own cupcake and a quarter of each other's dessert. Even though both tiny cakes were awesome, I knew I'd opt for the white cake and white icing every time.

"More wine?" I asked. We'd drunk the rhubarb with dinner, but I was anxious to try the blackberry. I also knew that a couple more glasses would maybe get Sky to talk about what had happened.

Sky nodded, his eyes just barely beginning to appear glassy. "Yes, please."

We sipped at our wine for a while and enjoyed the crackling fire in the pit as a cool, soft breeze played through the windchimes and ruffled our hair.

"Is there something wrong with me?" Sky whispered as he took a large swallow of his wine.

"What? Of course not. Why?" I frowned.

"Trent never wanted to be seen out in public with me, treated me like shit, *and* cheated on me. I'm so disgusted right now. For almost two years—if the boyfriend, *Dayton*, is to be believed. But there must be something wrong with me because Trent was out in public with Dayton. Why not with me? We basically look exactly the same. So, it's not like I'm more femme or whatever." Sky took a shuddery breath. "What's wrong with me?"

I took him in my arms and kissed the top of his head. "Listen, first of all, Trent is an asshole who doesn't deserve your time or energy. Whatever his reasoning, it's his issue and doesn't have anything to do with you. You're an amazing person and you didn't deserve any of what Trent put you through. Second, you don't know if this Dayton was telling the truth or not. He may have just been trying to get under your skin. Either way, they aren't your concern. Don't waste your thoughts on them. If Trent isn't already mistreating Dayton, he likely will be soon enough."

"I hate to think of another person stuck in my situation," Sky murmured.

"I get that. But Dayton isn't yours to worry about right now. Trent is toxic and you need to be away from him and anything to do with him." I ran my hand up and down his back.

Sky shivered. "Dayton said Trent called him for sex anytime I wouldn't put out or didn't satisfy him over the past two years." He paused and took a deep breath. "I never even suspected. And now I'm scared to death I might have something. I let Trent talk me into going bare pretty early in our relationship. I wasn't dumb enough to do it without both of us being tested, but it never occurred to me that he was cheating." Sky groaned. "God, I'm so fucking stupid. All those times he was *working late* or *getting overtime*—which he always blamed on me, saying he had to get money for covering my ass when I couldn't pay—he was likely out fucking Dayton." He huffed. "God, he always got so mad if I ever asked him to suck me off or let me top. He always told me that he only gave me the time of day way back then because I sucked dick so well. And he wasn't a sissy, bottom-boy. *You're the bottom* was always his response if I ever dared to hint around that I wanted to top."

Sky shifted and I squirmed with the thought of bottoming for him.

"Don't get me wrong. I love to suck dick and bottom. Definitely. But sometimes it's nice to change things up, you know? But Trent acted like blowing me was a disgusting chore and he *never* let me top. Told me to get a toy if I wanted to bury my dick in something."

"Sky, babe, Trent was a disgusting, hateful, selfish asshole and you need to forget about him. You are gorgeous, intelligent, and so damn amazing it sometimes makes it hard for me to breathe." I tipped his chin and brushed my lips over his. "If and when we ever decide to take things further, I'll be on my knees for you in a heartbeat. The thought of sucking you and having you in me absolutely takes my breath away. I usually lean a bit more to the top side of things, but if you want to top, I'll be more than willing to bottom."

Sky took a shaky breath and kissed me, slowly and softly. "I want it all. With you." He teased his tongue along my lips. "I wanna suck you and let you suck me. Wanna fuck you and be fucked. I'm going to slip my silk panties on and watch as you slide them from my body. I want you, Van."

I groaned and dipped my tongue into his mouth. "I want that, too. But not now. We've had too much wine. Charlie will be home soon. I need to know you're interested because of *us* and not because Trent and Dayton hurt you. And I'm so pissed at Trent right now, I can't say I'd be in it for the right reasons."

Sky nodded. "I get that." He shifted in my arms until we were horizontal on the lounge. Rocking our hips together, Sky kissed me deeply. "And I'm not comfortable doing anything more until I get tested."

I held the back of his head and kissed him long and hard, our stiff cocks pressed together as our bodies tangled together. "I'll go with you," I whispered.

Sky pulled back. "I wouldn't ask you to do that."

"You didn't ask. I offered. It's been close to a year since I was tested. I've always used condoms, but it's always better to be safe. We can go together." I scooted back on the lounge and Sky turned his back to me so he could face the fire.

"We should go in soon," he murmured.

"Yeah, just a few more minutes." I breathed against his neck.

What seemed like only a couple minutes later, I jerked awake when a hand nudged my arm.

"What the fuck, Van?" Charlie bit out in a hushed but angry tone.

I blinked my eyes as I came awake with Sky in my arms and the fire pit burning low. "Shhh," I warned. Extricating myself from the lounge and my cozy cocoon with Sky, I stood and pulled Charlie farther away. "He had a rough day. Trent was at the movies and gave him shit. Some guy Trent is dating cornered him in the bathroom and said he'd been fucking Trent for close to two years."

Charlie growled and ran a hand over his face.

"We got dinner and wine. He drank quite a bit, but it got him talking. We fell asleep. That's it." I brushed a hand through my hair. *Not for lack of wanting*, I thought.

"Sorry, didn't mean to jump to conclusions. I just don't want him hurt," Charlie said.

"And I do?" I huffed. "If anything ever happened between Sky and me it would be because we're both interested and on-board. I'd never purposely hurt him and I'm sure he'd never purposely hurt me." I glanced over to where Sky was moving on the couch. "Gonna get him to bed."

Charlie nodded. "Hey, Kendall and I were talking about camping this coming weekend. You think Sky would want to go? We could make it a whole group thing."

"We can ask him in the morning. Sounds fun." I gave my best friend a nod and went to where Sky was still sleeping.

Once I got a very groggy Skyler to his room, I guided him to the futon and let him fall to the cushion—we *had* to get him a bed. Or let him sleep in my bed. I groaned. Shoes, pants, and shirt came off quickly and efficiently, and I covered him right away with a thick quilt so as not to let my gaze linger on his chest, dark treasure trail, V lines, and thick package encased in soft cotton.

I kissed his head and whispered, "Sleep tight."

After a shower—yes, I jerked off to images of Sky—it was becoming a well-enjoyed habit—I crawled into bed and wondered what kind of fucked up mess Trent had to be to treat Sky the way he had. If I ever got the privilege to call Sky my boyfriend, I'd treasure him like he deserved.

NINE

SKY

MY PRINCIPAL, Mr. Frinks, clicked off the projector. "Folks, I gotta tell you. I planned for today be light as far as the presentation goes, but I'm coming down with something and we're going to end this even earlier than planned."

An excited murmur went through the staff gathered in the media center for our meeting. The day had been a scheduled professional development day and we'd done about four hours of training so far and my head was already spinning.

"You *are* welcome to stay and work in your rooms, but take my advice and enjoy the rest of your day. There are no pay raises or trophies for overworking yourself. If your fearless leader is going to go home and curl up in bed, you definitely have every right to take off." Mr. Frinks smiled and gathered up his materials. "Consider it an early Teacher Appreciation gift." He gave a slight wave and headed out the door.

A shuffle and low buzz began to travel through the staff. It soon turned into full-on laughing and giddiness as friends and colleagues planned to go out for lunch, shopping, and a variety of other things.

"Amazing what the gift of three and half hours can do for morale, huh?" My host teacher, Ms. Rose, smiled and picked up her notebook. "Since I know you're planned ahead and completely prepared, I'm making the executive decision that we both blow this joint. No arguments."

I chuckled and slid my computer into my bag. "No arguments here. This is amazing. I actually have an errand I need to run, so it works out perfectly."

We chatted a bit as we walked to the classroom to gather the rest of our belongings. Laughing about some of the funny things our students had done recently, making note of parents to contact, and agreeing on which tasks we'd each do at home, Ms. Rose and I headed out the door with our bags and smiles on our faces.

I couldn't help but laugh at how excited teachers got over a simple *you may leave early* statement. Mr. Frinks had just earned himself a gold star as far as bosses went. I definitely admired the man. He respected his staff, held them to high standards, and expected their best. But he also knew that family was important, life sometimes got in the way, and everyone needed a break from time-to-time.

I hopped into my car and tossed my bag in the passenger seat. I checked the time and decided I'd run home, get ready, and then see if Van wanted to go with me.

I'd settled into living with Charlie, Kendall, and Van fairly easily. We had a good dynamic, and I'd fallen back into my tight-knit friendship with both my brother and Van almost as if nothing had changed. Even though *a lot* had changed.

Things with Van and me were good. Great, actually. We weren't rushing things—in fact, I sometimes wanted to pull my hair out with how slow we seemed to be going—but we also didn't allow worry about Charlie's reaction or any other factors to keep us from exploring. We'd done a lot of making out and touching, but I was itching for more.

Charlie had planned a camping trip for the four of us. The original date got rained out, so we were doing attempt number two on the upcoming weekend.

But Trent's cheating had been hanging over my head and I needed to get rid of the dark cloud. I wasn't burdened by the cheating—okay, the cheating sucked and made me question a lot of shit about myself—but the actual cheating wasn't what bothered me the most. I was riddled with anxiety over the fact that Trent had knowingly exposed me to the possibility of a vast array of sexually transmitted infections.

I'd thought I was so smart making us both get tested before we had unprotected sex, but then I'd never considered that he'd cheat. Definitely stupid on my part. So, he'd been having sex with Dayton—and maybe others—and had exposed me to all of Dayton's sexual partners as well.

The only silver lining was that sex with Trent had dwindled to almost nothing over the past year or two, but that didn't mean I was immune to any STI he might have picked up from Dayton and whoever else.

I wanted to go camping and not have to worry. Maybe Van and I could sneak off and have our own fun. But I needed to know I was in the clear.

Van had said he'd go with me.

I had a free afternoon.

The clinic was open and took walk-ins.

I could have my results back before we left on Friday afternoon.

And if you've got something?

My gut churned. I'd deal with that if and when it happened.

I danced into the house and yelped when I saw Kendall in

the kitchen. "Oh shit! I didn't realize you were home. My bad."

"It's fine. I got sent home due to low numbers." She glanced at the clock on the microwave. "You're home early."

"Yeah, we got a rare afternoon off instead of dying in PD all day. I'm going to change and see if Van wants to go to the clinic with me." Kendall and Charlie knew the story of Trent and Dayton. As a medical professional, Kendall was very supportive, but also adamant that I get an STI screening.

"Remember, a *full* screening. Blood, urine, throat *and* rectal swab. Doing only a blood test or only a urine test doesn't cover everything. Better to do it all to cover all the bases." Kendall sipped her coffee. "I'm sure you and Van will both want to know you're clear of anything before getting down and dirty," she said with a smirk.

I swallowed thickly and studied my future sister-in-law with narrowed eyes. "I'm not sure I know what you're talking about," I lied.

Kendall snorted. "Yeah, okay. Charlie may be determined to believe that there's nothing between you and Van— actually, I think he *knows* there's something there, he just wants to think you guys will adhere to his childish and misguided attempts to keep you apart—but don't act like you and Van haven't been hot for each other since the night you came home."

I started to protest, but stopped and let out a long breath. I really loved how they'd welcomed me in and made me one of their own so quickly. And I loved Kendall to death. She was so good for Charlie. "I can neither confirm nor deny that information." I grimaced. "But if something *were* to happen between Van and me—and just know that it would be well-thought-out and very much consensual—do you think Charlie would flip out and never forgive us?"

Kendall took a final drink from her coffee mug and placed

it in the sink. "You and Van worry about you and Van. Let me handle Charlie. If and when something happens between you two—and let's face it, plenty has been happening and it's smart to take things slow—Charlie will likely flip out, but he's a reasonable man and I'll make sure he doesn't overreact."

I raised a brow.

"Okay, he'll definitely overreact, but I'll be there to bring him down. He won't be happy and he'll huff and puff, but eventually he'll hear me and see that you two are so good together. He loves you both so much. He'll come around." Kendall patted my shoulder. "Don't hold back on something with Van because of Charlie. You guys want to go slow? Fine. But do it because it's what you both want, not because your brother will go tits-up for a bit."

I laughed. "Thanks." I gave her a hug before rushing to my room.

I quickly changed into jeans and a t-shirt before stopping in the bathroom to check my hair. Catching my reflection in the mirror, I smiled slyly. It had been a long time since I'd done up my face. I didn't have the time or desire for a full-face—that was reserved for going out to gay bars—but makeup always made me feel powerful and I needed the extra boost that day.

After a quick swipe of eyeliner and a coat of mascara, I bit my lip and studied the man who stared back at me. I felt good. Would Van be okay with me wearing makeup? I shrugged. Better to find out he had an issue with it *now* than further down the road when my heart was even more involved.

I grabbed my phone, a smaller backpack which I threw my wallet and a bottle of water into, and my keys and hollered goodbye to Kendall. Skipping down the steps to my car, I chuckled at how happy I felt. Only a brief cloud of apprehension flitted through my head as I drove to Byrd and Badger; if Van didn't like my makeup and/or couldn't go to the clinic with me, I'd buck up and deal.

A few minutes later, I walked into the bar and immediately got butterflies when I saw Charlie and Van both glance my way—for two very different reasons. Charlie smiled and waved before catching the look Van was giving me and then my brother frowned. He shook his head, mumbling something to himself, as he attacked dirty tables with ferocity.

Van had yet to take his eyes off me and he stalked my way as if he had a purpose. "Come with me," he growled as he took my elbow and led me to the back room. When we walked into the small space that wasn't big enough for an office or storage space—it was more like a broom closet—Van quietly closed the door.

My heart thundered when the lock clicked.

"Hey," I croaked.

Van smirked and gave me the once over. "Hey yourself. You look fucking amazing."

I swallowed thickly. "Thanks. Wasn't sure how you felt about makeup..."

Van spun me around and pushed me against the door as his hot mouth attacked my lips. Our tongues danced and swirled as my arms snaked around Van's waist. He moaned into my mouth and rocked our hips together as I savored the flavor that was uniquely Van.

"I feel that you're sexy as fuck and whatever you want to wear is up to you. I like *you* for you, not what you wear," Van whispered gruffly against my ear.

I shivered and curled into his embrace. "Not even the silk panties?" I teased.

Van's breath caught and he chuckled. "Well, I haven't seen those with my own eyes, so I guess we'll have to see about that."

We made out a bit longer before I pulled back. "Oh, the reason I came here…"

"You mean you didn't just come to kiss me and send me back to work with a hard-on?" Van joked.

"No, I came to see if you could go with me to the clinic." I bit my lip. "I know you're probably busy, but I got out of school early today and thought it would be good to get it done before camping."

Van waggled his brows. "Got plans for the camping trip?"

I shrugged. "Would be nice not to have it hanging over my head."

"Sure thing. Let me tell Charlie I'm taking a long lunch."

"Will it cause a problem?" I frowned.

"Nah, it's not an issue," Van assured me.

In ten minutes, we were in my car and heading toward the clinic.

After a twenty-minute wait in the waiting room while we filled out paperwork, Van and I were called back separately. We'd already discussed that we'd request *full* screenings like Kendall had suggested.

Within thirty minutes, Van and I met in the waiting room with matching bandages on our arms.

"You good?" he asked.

"Yep, can't say any of it was difficult. *Really* glad they've moved away from the urethra swab." I shivered.

"Yeah, well. The anal swab wasn't bad, but I usually get at least dinner before anyone is that close to my ass," Van deadpanned.

I snorted. "They said results within forty-eight hours, right?" I asked as we climbed into the car.

"Yeah, they'll text us when the results are ready and we'll

log in to a secure site to get the information." Van took my hand as I pointed the car toward Byrd and Badger. "You super nervous about your results?"

I thought about the question for a bit. "Maybe a little. Little angry with myself—in addition to pissed at Trent—for not being more careful."

Van squeezed my hand. "You thought it was monogamous."

"Yeah," I sighed, "I think that's why it hurts. Will I ever be able to trust anyone again?"

Van ran a thumb over my hand. "I get the apprehension. If we're both clear of STI's and we decide to have sex, I completely understand if you're only comfortable with condoms." He leaned over the console and kissed me. "But I *have never* and *will never* cheat on anyone. *Ever.* I'm not that type of person."

"I didn't think Trent was either," I argued.

"Really?" Van raised a brow.

I started to protest, but clamped my mouth shut. "Yeah, okay, you have a very good point. In hindsight—and probably even in the very thick of the relationship—I can see how Trent never made himself out to be trustworthy." I pulled into the parking lot. "I trust you. You're my past, my present..." I paused.

"And your future, no matter what form of a relationship we take," Van promised.

"Since I'm home earlier than usual, I want to cook supper tonight. Will you be available?" I asked.

"Definitely. I think Charlie and Kendall are going out, but I would like to make a reservation for two at Café Skyler. Six o'clock?"

"Homemade chicken alfredo, garlic bread, and dessert. Sound okay?"

"Can't wait. I'll see you then." Van gave me a brief kiss

and climbed out of the car.

By the time six o'clock rolled around, I nervously ran my hands down my pants and glanced around the dining room table one last time.

The fettucine noodles seemed to have cooked nicely.

The alfredo sauce was mostly lump-free.

The chicken was my biggest concern. How did you know when chicken had cooked long enough? I didn't want to overcook it and have it turn out dry. It looked okay. Didn't it? I peered suspiciously at the chicken.

At least the garlic bread had been easy and smelled magnificent.

Dessert was definitely the best and I was excited to get to that part.

"Smells good," Van announced as he walked in behind me and took me in his arms. "Mmmm, the food too," he growled against my ear.

"Okay, let's eat before it gets cold," I suggested and we sat down.

We took turns dishing up the creamy pasta and chicken before choosing two pieces of garlic bread each.

My first bite had me frowning, making a sound of disgust, and spitting the whole thing into my napkin.

Van watched me with curiosity as he chewed for a second, but then his eyes grew wide and he too spat his food into his napkin. "So, the chicken may be a bit undercooked," he said with a soft, caring smile.

I grimaced. "A bit? It was almost still cold in the middle. I will *never* be able to forget the feeling of raw chicken between my teeth." I fought back a gag. "Oh God, I may barf."

"Hey, no harm, no foul," Van assured.

"Riiiight," I drawled. "Nothing like trying to give your boyfriend salmonella."

Van's brows shot up and I froze.

"Say that again," he ordered.

"Salmonella," I whispered.

"The other."

"Boyfriend?" I swallowed thickly. "Sorry, it just slipped out."

"Is that something you'd want? To be my boyfriend?"

"I mean, it fits. With the exception of faking it for Trent and that lady and her son—and not letting Charlie in on how close we've become—we treat each other like boyfriends. But I can see if you wouldn't want to be that serious with anyone you hadn't even done anything sexual with," I rambled.

Van stood and pulled me from my chair. "Shut up," he commanded and placed a bruising kiss against my lips. When we broke apart, breathless, he smiled. "There's no way sex with us won't be amazing. Just making out with you is crazy good. I'm down for being your boyfriend."

I frowned. "Do we tell Charlie?"

"Let's get through camping and the local business event, then we'll see where we stand and figure out the best way to tell him." Van tipped my chin up and brushed a kiss on my mouth. "Does that sound okay?"

I nodded, pretty sure I would have agreed to anything at that point because my head and heart were jumbled with all things Van. "Kendall said not to worry about Charlie and she'd take care of him."

"Perfect." Van glanced at the table. "My first thought was to just pick the chicken out, but raw chicken mixed with sauce and noodles is likely not safe. So, do we want to order-in or just skip straight to dessert?"

My stomach growled. "As excited as I am for you to try dessert, let's get actual food first. Burritos?"

"That sounds delish." Van pulled his phone out and we spent the next couple minutes placing our order from the *burritos as big as your head* place down the street.

While we waited for our food to be delivered, I wrapped my arms around Van's waist and mumbled into his chest. "Thank you for being so good about my fuck-up."

He pulled back and ducked his head to meet my eyes. "Seriously? It was a mistake. Not a big deal."

I huffed. "I feel stupid. I already feel like a total loser and freeloader, but screwing up dinner was a real slap in the face. Trent always said I had no business being in the kitchen; my best attributes were for the bedroom."

Van growled. "He's a fucking asshole and doesn't deserve a second of your thoughts. Did anyone ever teach you how to cook chicken?"

I shook my head. "My mom probably tried, but I was too busy flitting around and lost in my own head to pay much attention to that shit when I was younger." I cuddled into Van's warm embrace. "You're seriously not mad at me? Not going to berate me for my stupidity and wasting the food? Laugh at me for the rest of forever about raw chicken?"

Van raised a brow in a *really* look. "Is there anything about me that makes you think I'd ever do any of that?"

I smiled softly and my whole body seemed to float. "No," I shook my head. "Even when we were little, and Charlie was giving me a hard time about things, you never made fun of me or treated me like I was stupid."

"And I never will. It's just not in my nature. Trent clearly has issues and it would be great if he someday could get help for himself, but he's not your worry. I'm not Trent. Charlie isn't Trent. Your family isn't Trent. We all love you, support you, and want what's best for you."

A knock at the door broke the moment and Van went to retrieve our burritos.

Thirty minutes later, we both moaned as we flopped back against the couch after stuffing ourselves with burrito deliciousness.

"I made strawberries for dessert," I murmured through my food coma. "The easy but delicious kind where you just cut them up and sprinkle a bit of sugar? So good. Trent never let me buy strawberries, always said they were too pricey for just some average fruit he couldn't make anything amazing from."

Van scowled. "Oh, um, I'm so full. Not sure I could eat anything else right now."

"Just a couple bites. The sweetness will cut the spiciness of the burritos," I said.

"Don't you want to take the strawberries to school tomorrow? Share with your colleagues or eat them all for yourself?" Van suggested.

I sat up and stretched. "Oh, there are *plenty*. I'll likely be able to eat them the rest of the week." I gave Van a shy smile. "I'd just kinda like you to taste something I made that isn't undercooked or could potentially give you food poisoning."

Van smiled weakly and gave an odd little chuckle. "Just a couple bites. That's seriously all I can handle."

"Come to the kitchen," I said as I gathered up the trash. "Dessert and then I have to get some school work done before bed."

Once in the kitchen, I pulled a large bowl of strawberries from the refrigerator. "I always loved strawberries this way, but I don't remember Mom ever fixing them. Or at least not more than a couple times. I love how sweet they are with such little effort. The hardest part is cutting the stems off and slicing the berries." I got two very small bowls from the cabinet and scooped strawberries into each.

"Oh, that's plenty. Just a couple bites," Van warned.

I handed him a bowl and spoon. "I hope they're good. Surely I can't screw up strawberries."

Van took a bite and chewed slowly. "They taste amazing."

I beamed and took my own bite. "Oh, they do! They're so good. I think I'll turn into a strawberry by the end of this week. I'll make sure we always have them on the grocery list so we can have strawberries all the time." I took another bite and savored the sweet tartness of the berries.

"Don't want to have too much of a good thing." Van cleared his throat and sat his bowl in the sink. He coughed and sniffed. "Those tasted great." He cleared his throat again.

The backdoor opened and Charlie and Kendall walked in from their dinner date.

"What's up?" Charlie asked.

I laughed. "Well, I almost killed us with raw chicken in the chicken alfredo, so we ordered burritos and I fixed strawberries for dessert."

Charlie frowned and glanced at Van.

Van shook his head and cleared his throat.

Kendall put a hand to her mouth as her eyes grew wide.

"Did you eat them?" Charlie demanded of Van.

Van sniffed, cleared his throat, coughed. "Let it go, Charlie. It's fine." He cleared his throat again.

I glanced around the group and immediately realized they all knew something that I didn't. "Wait, let what go? What's fine? Van?"

Van took a deep breath and rubbed at his lips before clearing his throat again. "Don't worry about it. Dinner and dessert were great. You should probably get busy on school work. I'll finish up in here. Maybe a movie before bed?"

Charlie rolled his eyes.

Kendall cocked her head in a mix of *aww, so cute* and *what an idiot.*

I crossed my arms. "No, I want to know what's going on."

Charlie went to the cabinet where the over-the-counter medications were kept and tossed a bottle to Van. "Take it. And tell him."

Van shook his head and cleared his throat.

"Tell me *what*?" I demanded.

"Van is allergic to strawberries," Charlie said.

I gasped and my eyes nearly bugged out of my head. "What? No. You're not, right?" I glanced at Van who was swallowing pills with a glass of water.

Van winced. "I am. But I only took a few bites, it's not too bad. Took some antihistamines." He shook the bottle. "I'll be good as new in a couple minutes."

"Van!" I cried. "You're fucking allergic to strawberries and didn't tell me? You let me basically force-feed you something that could have killed you?"

"The reactions aren't really *that* bad and I only ate a few. It's all good."

"It's *not* all good," I wailed. "Oh my God, first possible salmonella and now anaphylaxis!" I dropped my chin and held my head in my hands.

Van came over and tipped my chin up. "Stop," he whispered. "My lips and throat get itchy, that's about it. You were so bummed over the chicken and so excited about the strawberries, I couldn't help but take a couple bites. I didn't want to disappoint you." When he looked as if he'd lean in and kiss me, he paused. "I took some medicine. I'll be fine. Just probably better not eat any from now on."

"How did you not know he was allergic?" Charlie demanded.

I shrugged. "I don't know. No one ever told me."

"It's why we hardly ever had strawberries as kids. Van *loves* strawberries, but can't have them." Charlie put the bottle of antihistamines back in the cabinet.

"I'm sorry! I was little, I probably didn't hear it talked

about or didn't understand it. I just knew I liked strawberries and wondered why we didn't eat them much." I pouted. "I feel so bad."

Charlie turned to Van. "You're an idiot. Why didn't you just tell him you can't eat strawberries?"

"He was so upset about the chicken. I figured a couple bites wouldn't hurt." Van cleared his throat. "See? Already a bit better."

Charlie rolled his eyes, glanced between the two of us, mumbled something and left the room shaking his head.

Kendall placed a hand on Van's shoulder. "That could have been dangerous. No more strawberries, no matter how excited Sky is about them."

"I'll never feed him strawberries again!" I promised.

When they were gone, I fell into Van's arms.

"I'm so sorry. Please don't *ever* put yourself in danger for me. I *never* want to think that I've hurt you in any way," I mumbled against his chest.

"It was probably dumb of me, but I won't do it again." Van kissed the top of my head. "For what it's worth, I do *love* strawberries and those few bites were absolute bliss."

"Until your throat started to close up," I deadpanned.

Van snorted. "It's not that bad. My lips itch and get a little numb. My throat gets itchy. That's all."

"Can't allergic reactions get worse over time?" I demanded. "Don't ever eat something you can't have or don't like for me again. I'll never forgive myself."

"Okay, okay. It's all over now. I'm sorry."

After dishes, showers, and school work—Van was so damn cute helping me cut out colored shapes—we decided on a movie.

"As much as I'd really like to cuddle up on my bed with you," Van said as he nuzzled my cheek, "I think the couch is safer. For now."

We kinda watched the movie as we kissed and cuddled—keeping an ear out for Charlie to walk down the hall—and I went to bed with a smile on my face despite what had been a potentially disastrous evening.

TEN

VAN

SKY and I decided we'd check our test results together in case either of us got news we weren't expecting. Two days before the camping trip—and the weekend's weather promised to be amazing this time—Sky and I sat on the futon in his little room and punched in the individual codes we were given.

I held my breath as the information loaded. I wasn't super worried about my own results, but I was concerned for Sky's health. Trent cheating had put Skyler at a great risk.

Sky sighed. "All negative except the HSV-1, which I knew about. You?"

My shoulders relaxed a bit and I scanned my phone screen. "Same. Just the HSV-1. And I've had that since long before I began getting STI screenings."

"Yeah, I remember we both would get cold sores as kids. My dad and Charlie don't get them, but my mom and I do. Weird. I hate those things." Sky flopped back against the cushion and let out a long breath. "Knew I was worried, didn't realize *how* worried I was until I saw all of those negatives. Even with cures and treatments—and we're lucky to live in a time period when so many advancements are being made—I was still nervous."

I put my arm around his shoulder and pulled him close. "I get it. I was worried for you."

"Would it have made a difference? Between us, I mean." Sky turned toward me.

I shook my head. "No. We would have dealt with the treatment and whatever extra precautions were needed. Even now, any precautions you want, I'm good. Clear tests don't automatically mean we *have* to jump right into unprotected sex. I definitely understand if you have hesitations."

Sky was quiet for a moment. "I think with anyone else—everyone else—I'd be scared and constantly worried they were going to do the same thing to me that Trent did." He leaned over and kissed me. "But you?" He shook his head. "You've had my back since we were kids. I know you'd never put me at risk."

"I hereby solemnly swear to keep my mouth off your dick at even the slightest sign of a cold sore on my lip," I stated, trying to keep a straight face.

Sky laughed. "I was actually talking about cheating, you big goof, but same for me. Do you have the antiviral pills to take? My dentist gave them to me and they really help to shorten the duration and lessen the pain."

"I do. Dr. Saun—that's my dentist—gave me some about a year ago when she saw I had a cold sore during one of my routine cleanings. I never knew dentists could prescribe that kind of medication, but I'm really glad she did."

Sky's eyes lit up. "I go to Dr. Saun, too."

"No shit? That's kinda weird. We all had the same dentist as kids, but the fact that we ended up at the same dental office as adults is almost freaky."

"Well, you know what they say about friends going to the same dentist." Sky smiled and winked.

"What's that?" I raised a brow.

"Friends who go to the same dentist are destined for great things," Sky teased.

"Oh, is *that* what they say?" I nuzzled against his ear. "I thought the saying was *friends who go to the same dentist often find themselves in sexy situations on camping trips.*"

Sky waggled his brows. "Like I said, *great things.*"

We spent the rest of the evening packing, doing school stuff—okay, Sky did school stuff and I helped where I could—and watching random television. I ran down to Byrd and Badger to help Charlie for a couple hours and then the three of us watched a movie before bed. Sky and I sat on the couch. It was getting harder and harder to avoid touching Sky in front of Charlie and I was *this close* to telling Charlie to fuck right off with his *don't mess shit up with my brother* ridiculousness.

Camping and the business event first. Then we'd tell him. He could flip out all he wanted. I'd *make* him understand how much I loved Sky.

My heart stopped and then beat at quadruple speed. *Loved Sky?* With any other guy I'd dated that thought would have sent me running for the hills. But with Sky? It was almost as easy as breathing. Of course, I loved him. I'd loved him since he was born in one way or another. Despite our relationship being mostly friendship and brotherly when we were younger, we'd fallen easily into the *more* category and I was completely confident and comfortable with my love for Sky.

And I wasn't going to hide it from Charlie for much longer.

I didn't want to hurt my best friend, but I wouldn't deny Sky's and my happiness just to keep Charlie content.

As soon as Sky walked in from school on Friday afternoon, we all four piled in the truck Charlie had borrowed from his dad and headed to the campsite.

"Did you get all your work done ahead of time so you can totally relax this weekend?" I asked Sky as we settled into the backseat of the extended cab truck.

He smiled brightly. "Yep. Took a lot of extra effort, but I was able to pre-plan throughout this week so my weekend is free. And Ms. Rose took home everything I'd normally do over the weekend and told me to have a good time."

"Perfect. No phones, no work, just fresh air and fun." I slid my hand across the seat and took Sky's.

After a nervous glance to the driver's seat where Charlie was sitting, Sky smiled slyly and gave my hand a squeeze.

About an hour into the three hour drive, Sky laughed aloud out of the clear blue.

"What?" I asked.

He shook his head. "Hey, guys," he directed his words mostly to Charlie and Kendall. "I had absolutely no plan to ever tell you this—not that I'm ashamed or embarrassed, just that you don't have any real reason to know it—but then I realized that it *could* potentially cause misunderstandings and issues down the road."

Charlie's raised brows met mine in the rearview mirror and Kendall turned slightly in her seat.

"Um, I have a thing for wearing silk. Mostly silk panties. So, Kendall, if you ever see any in the laundry that you don't recognize, don't go ballistic thinking Charlie is cheating. They're mine." Sky chuckled. "I usually hand wash, but I had this awful thought of what would happen if you found strange silk panties and thought they belonged to another woman. I mean, I mostly buy pairs made for men, but they look pretty much like ladies silk panties, so I didn't want it to cause a problem."

Charlie stared at his brother in the mirror for so long I worried about our safety on the road. "Absolutely fantastic. You think you can tell my fiancée you wear silk panties and she's not going to try to get me into a pair? Van once mentioned a cock ring and she had one of those bought so fast I didn't know what hit me."

"Hey," Kendall exclaimed with a slap to his shoulder. "That thing is magic. You like it."

"Not the point." He turned toward her and attempted to keep a stern face. "Just because my brother wears silk doesn't mean I'd like it."

"Never know unless you try," Kendall suggested with an impish smile.

"Also never know if you like ass play either. You know, a bit of fingering, rimming, pegging? All could make your ass very happy," Sky teased.

"My ass is perfectly happy. Don't give her ideas," Charlie bit out, only half serious in his irritation.

"Is your ass looking for attention, babe?" Kendall joked. "Why didn't you tell me? You know I'm all about exploration and pleasure. We'll need to add some items to our shopping list."

"Oh God," Charlie groaned. "Thanks for that, Squirt. I think I'd almost rather she'd found your damn panties and accused me of cheating."

We all laughed. The teasing and joking continued for a bit until Charlie pulled off at a gas station.

"Fuel, drinks, snacks, and a pee break," Charlie announced.

"Oh good, I need to piss," Sky said as he hopped from the

truck. "I think this is one those ask for the key type places."
He headed toward the little store.

With one single thought—and it wasn't about using the
restroom—I went around the side of the building. The
bathrooms were on the very back of the store—not exactly
the safest area. I sat on the little concrete wall across from
the doors and waited for Sky.

In a few moments, his head hesitantly popped around the
corner and he jumped. "Oh my God, you scared the shit out
of me." Sky held a hand to his heart before shaking a large
license plate with a key attached.

I laughed at the sight and stood. When Sky moved to
unlock the bathroom door, I glanced around to be sure we
were alone and moved to stand flush against his back. Loving
the way Sky immediately melted into me, I whispered against
his ear, "Open the door."

As soon as the door opened, I pushed him inside and
slammed the door behind us, locking it with a click. I
removed the key from Sky's hand and placed it on the sink.

Sky's fiery eyes laughed as he wrapped his arms around
my waist. "What makes you think I'm the type of boy to get
freaky in a gas station bathroom."

"Nothing." I glanced around at the disgusting bathroom.
"Because *I'm* not the type of boy to get freaky in a gross place
like this." With a hand at the nape of his neck, I pulled him
in for a deep, slow kiss. "But I couldn't go the rest of the trip
without asking a question."

"Asking a question? Is that what you're doing?" Sky
kissed me again, sliding his tongue against mine and
moaning as he took hold of my hips and pressed our semi-
hard cocks together.

"I would be, if my *boyfriend* wasn't distracting me," I
mumbled against his mouth. Pulling from the contact, I

cupped his face in my hands. "Do you have silk panties on right now?"

Sky's eyes danced. "Maybe." He shrugged with a fluttering of his lashes. "Only one way to find out."

I growled and moved in to devour his mouth as my hands slid to the waistband of his joggers. Without hesitation, I delved under the elastic and slipped my hands down to cup his ass. The slight scratch of lace and then the smooth slide of silk under my skin told me all I needed to know. "Fuuuuck," I groaned into Sky's mouth. "You're going to kill me. How am I supposed to ride two more hours *and* sleep in a separate tent knowing your ass is covered in skimpy, silky panties."

"Mmm, my ass cupped in silk *is* amazing, but wait until you see how good my cock looks encased in it. Love the look of my balls and dick all snug under the material." Sky whimpered and dropped his head back, exposing his neck to my kisses.

"We gotta get away on our own. I want to see you, wanna see your hard cock strain against the material as your cum wets the silk," my words were gruff as my lips skimmed his hot skin.

"Fuck, Van. I don't want to wait anymore. We've *got* to do more than kissing and some touching. I need to feel you, wanna come for you," Sky answered breathlessly.

Realizing we'd been in the bathroom for a bit, I reluctantly pulled away from Sky. "We will. Tonight. Promise." I adjusted my dick. "Now, I've got to figure out how to take a piss with a boner."

Sky laughed. "I'll stand guard. Wouldn't be good for Charlie to find us in the bathroom together comparing hard-ons. But make it quick, I really do need to pee."

A couple minutes later, Sky and I walked from around the back of the building and nearly ran into Charlie.

"Oh, here's the key." Sky handed the jangly license plate over. "I'm going to get drinks and snacks."

Charlie eyed us with suspicious eyes, but he took the key and rounded the corner.

Sky chuckled, but it held very little humor. "How mad do you think he's going to be? Like kick me out mad? Never speak to me mad?" His smile faded.

"If anything, he'll be the most upset with me." I paused. "I don't think Charlie has it in him to kick us out or never speak to us. He'll throw a fit. And I'm not saying he doesn't have some valid points, but I really think he'll get over it. I just don't like to upset anyone and it will definitely upset him." I bumped my shoulder against Sky's as we stood in front of the soda fountains. "I'm in this though. If he kicks one or both of us out, I say we get our own place."

Sky turned wide eyes my way. "For real?"

I winced. "Sorry. It's not really my place to ask you to leave your brother when you just got there. And that's probably moving way too fast."

He smiled softly. "No, it's nice to know we'd have that option if it came down to it. What would it do to your business relationship?"

I took a deep breath and put together a Styrofoam cup of Pepsi with the crunch ice. "We're borrowing trouble. Let's just see how things play out."

Sky worried his lower lip, but nodded before making his own large cup of Pepsi.

We each bought chips and candy for the trip, a couple hot dogs to eat right then, and headed to the truck where Charlie was impatiently waiting.

"Took you long enough," he groused. "We've got two hours still to drive. I want to get the tents set up before dark."

"Um, Charlie? I think this one has seen its last campout." Sky held up two completely broken tent poles and the tent with a huge hole in the side.

"What the fuck?" Charlie growled. "How the hell did that happen?" He yanked the tent poles from Sky and examined them as if he'd be able to magically repair them with his angry eyes. After tossing them to the ground with disgust, he grabbed the tent and held it up to study the hole—which was basically the whole side of the tent just shredded—and growled again as he threw it to the ground. "That's the thanks I get for letting those fuckers at the bar borrow my tent. And they returned it this way? Didn't even tell me?" He kicked at the poles. "What the fuck are we going to do now?"

Kendall walked up and placed a hand on his shoulder. "Babe, we still have two tents. There's no issue."

Charlie shook his head. "No. No, no, no," he grumbled. "You," he jabbed a finger in my direction, "will have to sleep on the ground. No, you can have the bed of the truck."

"Charlie!" Kendall exclaimed. "There's no reason for anyone to have to sleep on the ground or in the truck. We have two full-size tents; each can comfortably sleep four people."

My best friend's eyes were wild as he glanced from Kendall to me to Sky. "Van, you can sleep with me. Kendall and Sky can share a tent."

Kendall's eyes grew wide and she huffed before gripping Charlie's arm and dragging him off to the privacy of the woods.

"Wow, we really have him worried, huh?" I frowned.

"Charlie likes things to go exactly as *he* plans them. Finding out his tent is broken *and* that we'll need to share a space—when he's already terrified we're going to break each other's hearts—is probably about to short-circuit him right now." Sky gathered up all of the broken tent pieces and took them to the truck. "Hopefully Kendall can set him straight. Pretty sure she wasn't planning on sharing a tent with me this weekend."

Several minutes later, after Sky and I had set up the two remaining tents and started to gather kindling for the fire, Kendall and Charlie reappeared.

"Sorry, I freaked out," Charlie grumbled and kicked at the dirt. "Thanks for getting the tents set up."

With the air cleared—although, there was still a trace of tension—the four of us set to work unloading the rest of the truck, building the base for a fire, securing the food, putting drinks in the cooler, and setting up chairs around the middle of our little area. We'd opted for an area farthest out so there wouldn't be a chance of many people being around.

"We're going to hike up that hill," Kendall said with a thumb thrown over her shoulder. "Says it's about an hour up and an hour down. We can make some food when we return."

"Why don't you guys come with us," Charlie suggested, almost desperately.

"Nooo," Kendall drawled in frustration. "This trip isn't about a foursome the *whole* time." She took Charlie's hand and pulled him over to load their backpacks.

Sky and I both cracked open some water bottles and took a seat around the not-yet-burning fire.

"We'll wait about an hour and then get the fire going," I called out to Charlie and Kendall as they disappeared down the trail leading into the woods.

"Thank God for Kendall," Sky muttered as we watched them leave. "So, we've got at least two hours." He winked and glanced over his shoulder at the tent that was now *ours* for two nights. "Whatever shall we do?"

With mischief in both our eyes, we scrambled from our chairs and dove into the tent. I made quick work of zipping up the flap in the large tent while Sky spread our sleeping bags.

"Come here," I growled and pulled him close, my lips meeting his in a hot, desperate kiss. When we finally broke apart, I whispered against his mouth, "What do you want to do?"

"Set an alarm for ninety minutes. Then get naked," Sky demanded.

I hesitated even as I set an alarm on my phone. "You sure?"

"Not full-on sex. Not here, not our first time," Sky explained. "But if I don't get to see you and touch you *now*, I'm going to explode."

I stripped my shirt over my head and pushed my jeans down. "Oh, you're going to explode. I guarantee that."

Sky shed his shirt, but paused before removing his pants.

Our eyes met and I knew he was stopping to be sure I was watching.

"Let me see," I ordered.

He turned away from me, watching me over his shoulder as he slowly shimmied his pants over his silk-covered ass. I barely noticed when he kicked his pants aside because my eyes were glued to his gorgeous ass, cupped in pale pink silk, with just the barest curve of his cheeks peeping from below.

"Turn around," I growled.

Sky made a show of swinging his hips as he turned to face me, his lip between his teeth, a fiery flash of desire in his eyes. And a silky bulge calling to me.

"So damn gorgeous," I whispered and reached for him.

A look of uncertainty crossed Sky's face. "You're okay with it? It's not just a turn-on now when we're hidden away and you'll be angry about it later?"

I pulled him close. "Never. You're perfect in anything and everything you ever decide to wear. Cotton, silk, lace, or bare; clear face, glossy lips, or glammed up like a movie star. None of that matters to me as long as you're happy." I held him tight as he buried his face in my chest.

"Thank you," he whispered. "What do you want to do?"

I shook my head. "This is your show, babe. You're in control. I'm thinking later, maybe blowjobs in the woods. But right now? You tell me."

"I wanna touch you. Wanna come and feel you come." Sky shuddered against me.

With my arms still around him, I lowered us to the floor of the tent and rolled so that Sky was on top. We shimmied out of our underwear—laughing at how it would have been easier to do that before lying down—and gasped when our rock-hard, bare cocks and heated skin came into contact.

"Fuck, Sky," I groaned as pleasure rippled through me with the touch.

Sky pushed up on his hands and glanced between us where our throbbing dicks leaked and rubbed together. "Wanna get off like this," he whispered. "He said this was for sissies and didn't count as real sex, but I want to feel us together and watch you come."

"Put him out of your head," I demanded. "We can get off however you want. *Real sex* is whatever we make it, whatever we want it to be. I wanna see you rub yourself off on me, wanna take our cocks in my hand and jack us both until we come."

Sky whimpered and rocked into me, the friction between our hard lengths nearly setting me on fire.

Letting Sky set the pace, I loosely held his hips and grunted with each thrust of his cock against mine. "Feels so good," I rasped.

"Touch me, jack us off," Sky demanded as he rolled to the side and pulled me to face him.

With a groan, I took his perfect cock along with mine and stroked our shafts in my fist. Thumbing my own slit, I captured his gasp with my lips as I smeared my precum over his leaking head. Bringing my thumb to my mouth, I licked our mixed flavors before offering it to him.

Sky greedily sucked my thumb and tongued away our precum as a jolt of pleasure traveled through me. I grunted before gripping our cocks again and jacking us to a rhythm that was only ours. Only Sky and me.

Sky began to pump his hips faster, his breaths coming hard and quick. "So close, Van."

"Come for me," I whispered in his ear. "Wanna feel you spill on me, feel your hot cum mix with mine."

That was all it took before Sky threw his head back and groaned as his body shook with orgasm. With his pulsing dick against mine, I watched him for a brief moment before I lost it and shot thick ropes of white over my fist.

We laid together for several minutes while catching our breaths and just enjoying the afterglow of what we'd done.

"That was good, right?" Sky murmured against my chest.

I kissed the top of his head. "That was amazing." In truth, no sexual encounter had *ever* been so good for me. Was it because Sky and I just fit? Was it because I loved him in a way I could never love the others? I honestly didn't care what the reason; I wasn't letting him go.

"It's never been like that for me," he whispered. "Ever. Even before Trent."

"We're good together," I answered with a kiss to his temple. "Never been that good for me, either," I admitted.

"Shit, we need to clean up," Sky grumbled. "I'd rather not spend the weekend covered in dried cum."

I laughed and rolled to the side to rummage in my bag. With a huff of triumph, I produced a package of baby wipes.

"Van, my gentle-giant to the rescue as usual," Sky teased.

We spent a few minutes wiping ourselves off and getting dressed before tossing the used wipes in a trash bag.

Sky glanced at my phone. "Perfect timing. We've got thirty minutes to make out before we need to start the fire."

I wrapped my arms around him and lowered my head for a long, deep kiss.

Several moments later, we broke for air with gleaming eyes and happy smiles.

"Will you go to the woods with me later? Either tonight or tomorrow?" I held his hips and pressed our bodies together. "Maybe blowjobs in the woods aren't the most conventional, but I want my mouth on you so badly. *Need* to taste you."

Sky pulled back in shock. "You want to suck me off?"

I cocked my head. "Um, duh? Been wanting to taste you for weeks. Why? Do you not like blow jobs?" No way would I force him to do something he didn't enjoy.

"No, no," Sky shook his head, "it's not that. It's just Trent hardly ever gave head. *You're the cocksucker in this relationship* was his go-to."

"But you like it?"

Sky nodded. "Definitely."

"Lucky for you, I'm just as greedy about getting a cock in *my* mouth as I am about getting my cock in *a* mouth—equal opportunity here—so you better believe that your days of going without are long over," I murmured my promise against his ear and smiled as he shivered.

"Can't wait. Seriously, haven't been sucked in so long, I'll likely blow within thirty seconds," Sky warned.

"No worries, we've got plenty of time to work on that stamina."

We left the tent and got the fire going before preparing the little table we'd brought with food items. Hot dogs, hamburgers, marshmallows, condiments, we had it all.

As Sky and I settled in to enjoy the fire and wait for Charlie and Kendall, we popped open cans of Byrd and Badger cider.

"Hey, earlier when Kendall mentioned a foursome, that got me thinking," Sky said conversationally.

I nearly spit out my drink. Instead, I choked and jerked my head his way. "You want a foursome?"

Sky chuckled. "Not a foursome. But a threesome is something I've always been interested in. Trent refused because he was scared I'd leave him for the other guy. Said me wanting a threesome just proved I was a slut who wanted to cheat."

I coughed again and took a swig of cider in hopes of calming myself. "So, like a triad or throuple type thing?"

"No, no. Nothing romantic with the third. Just sex; a fantasy I'd like to make happen. Would you ever be interested?" Sky raised a brow as he took a sip.

"If it was just a kink or fantasy type thing, yeah, I'd totally be down." I nodded. "I'm not made up the right way to be okay with sharing you romantically—okay, I need to rephrase that—at this point in time, I can't see myself ever being able to be romantically involved with more than one man. I'm not saying *never*, but I know how my jealousy gets." I took another drink. "But adding a third just to play around? Hell, yeah."

"How does one even find a person to do that? *Hi, I'm Sky. Want to fuck around with me and boyfriend?* Or put up flyers on campus? *Want to have a threesome? Call this number.*" Sky rolled his eyes.

We both laughed and finished off our drinks.

"I'll ask around quietly. There are a few guys at work who may be interested or know someone who is," I offered.

Sky's eyes grew wide. "*Quietly* would be the operative word here. Definitely don't need Charlie finding out."

I snorted. "For sure." My mind tried to process just how pissed Charlie would be if Sky and I had a threesome with a Byrd and Badger employee. Holy shit, it would be an epic meltdown.

"I want to lay it out up front that it's just a fantasy and just for fun. Nothing more. I'd prefer no kissing except between us—but that might change during the heat of the moment—and condoms are a must in a threesome situation, at least for me." Sky rattled off his requirements.

"Babe, it's your show. You set up the parameters." I shifted in my seat. "Don't get me wrong, the idea of watching you be fucked by another cock, or burying myself in your ass while you fuck someone else, has me all kinds of turned on," I admitted. "But I don't want to set up the threesome until after you and I have had at least a few go-rounds in bed. Not blowjobs in the woods and hand jobs in a tent. I want your body as *only mine* for a while."

A brief tension crossed Sky's face.

"What? What's wrong?" I asked.

Sky shrugged. "Trent always treated me like his property. Like I was only good enough to keep around for sex. He almost always refused to give me head. And he *never* let me top. *But you're the bottom* was a phrase I heard over and over in our three years together." He took a deep breath and a storm passed through his eyes. "But I'm more than that. I'm a man, a teacher, a son, a brother, a friend. I'm not just some hole to fuck."

Not caring that Charlie and Kendall could walk up any moment, I stood and pulled Sky from his chair before wrapping him in my arms. "There will *never* be a time when I look at you as *just* or *only* anything. You're my friend, my boyfriend, and an amazing person. I'd be happy the rest of my life if you only ever wanted to top; for real, I'd be completely down with it. Don't you *ever* think that you're required to be a certain way for me. You are not *the bottom*—as if it's your place in life—and I'll smash my fist through that prick's face if I ever see him again."

Sky shuddered in my arms and nodded against my chest. "God, I love you so much."

He froze.

I froze.

And then I smiled and tipped his chin so I could look in his eyes.

"Sorry, that slipped. I mean, I *do* love you, but not like…" Sky paused with a frown. "No, that's a lie. I'm not going to lie. I know it's early and things could get messed up with Charlie, but I don't care. I've loved you in one way or another since we were kids, and I love you romantically—and as a partner—now. I don't expect you to feel the same, but I won't deny how I feel."

I kissed him softly—and then not-so-softly—before grinning from ear-to-ear. "I love you. I'm not sure exactly when our friendship love and brotherly-type love morphed into something more, but I do. I love you." I kissed him again. "Now, as much as I'd love to spend the rest of our evening making out and declaring our love, your brother is going to be back soon."

"Do you think Charlie will accept us easier if he knows we truly love each other?" Sky asked as he retrieved another cider and returned to his seat.

"I don't know." I shrugged. "And I honestly don't care. I love you, you love me. Charlie will need to get that through his thick head and realize that we're not going to hurt each other and leave him in the middle. What we have is more than that."

Charlie and Kendall returned about ten minutes later—both looking well-sexed, so I assumed they'd taken advantage of an empty woods like we'd done with an empty campsite. Thank you, Kendall.

We spent the rest of the night eating, drinking, laughing, and building memories.

ELEVEN

SKY

"WE'RE GOING FOR A HIKE," Van told Charlie and Kendall, who were packing up their fishing gear and heading to a nearby lake.

"Why not come fishing with us?" Charlie asked with a scowl. "Thought this was a family trip."

"We'll catch up with you guys later. I'm sure you'll be a few hours fishing, at least. Sky wanted to check out the trail," Van explained as he packed his backpack with snacks and water.

I smiled and attempted to look innocent. "I haven't been hiking in forever. We're trying the beginner trail so I don't kill myself. But I want to take pictures to show to my kids." I held up my phone and hoped I wasn't radiating *I'm getting head out in the woods* vibes.

Charlie grumbled something.

Kendall gave us a wink and threw her bag over her shoulder. "We'll be at the lake. Have a nice hike."

Once they'd taken off toward the lake, Van chuckled. "Damn, I feel like two horny teenagers trying to sneak one past their parents." He hefted his backpack up onto his back. "You ready?"

About thirty minutes into our hike, we found a gorgeous little secluded spot off the main trail that was hidden by a grove of trees. I'd taken about fifty pictures as we walked and was ready for a break.

"Let's stop here," I said. "I'm not too sweaty yet," I waggled my brows suggestively.

Van dropped his bag and wrapped me in his arms.

I sighed. I swore I'd never get tired of Van holding me.

"A little sweat isn't a turn-off for me," he growled against my ear as he pushed me a bit farther into the wooded area. "I don't think there are many people out here, but be quiet just the same."

I watched in wonderment as Van worked the button on my pants and pushed them down just far enough to expose my already semi-hard cock. I seriously couldn't believe that he *wanted* to give me head. "Sorry, went with plain cotton today since we're hiking," I mumbled like an idiot.

Van dropped to his knees and nuzzled his nose against my abdomen, ran his tongue along my V-line, and placed kisses on my length. "Don't ever apologize. I want you any and every way I can get you. Silk, lace, cotton, polyester, spandex, as long as I get to remove it and see your body, I'm down."

I chuckled. "Polyester and spandex, huh? I'll keep that in mind."

Van took his time, but eventually pulled the waistband of my underwear low under my balls and spent several moments nuzzling his nose against me, as if savoring the moment. With a fiery gleam in his eyes, he glanced up at me as he took my shaft in his hand and smeared my pre-cum against his lips. "I like it hard," he whispered. "Wanna gag on this cock. Wanna feel you fuck my face until you're coming down my throat."

I whimpered and nodded, desperate to feel his lips around me. I nearly lost all semblance of control when Van's tongue swirled around my head and teased my slit before his hot mouth engulfed me.

We started slow, but within a few moments, Van's fingers dug into my hips as he guided me to thrust hard and fast into his mouth. I worried momentarily that it was too hard, but the sexy way Van stared up at me, my cock sliding in and out of his mouth as his eyes watered, told me he was enjoying it as much as I was.

My balls drew up tight just as Van's hands pushed my pants below my ass and delved between my cheeks to tease my hole. The press of his finger against my entrance was all it took to send me over the edge. I watched, mesmerized, as my cock pulsed over and over into Van's greedy mouth. He swallowed what I gave him and wiped his mouth with the back of his hand. Then he stood, and pressed his hard length against me as he devoured my mouth and pushed his tongue —covered in my cum—into my mouth, and I whimpered. Pulling back, I gasped, "My turn."

I spun Van around to lean against the tree and dropped to my knees. Never taking my eyes from his, I yanked his pants and underwear down, and groaned when his cock sprung free. I took him in my fist and stroked as I peppered kisses against his abdomen and his groin. The scent of man—of *Van* —nearly short-circuited my senses and I licked my lips before taking his entire length deep to the back of my throat.

"Wanna go slow," Van murmured. "Play with my balls and suck me slow and deep."

I was totally on board with that. While I definitely had no qualms with hard and fast, Trent had only ever wanted to use me as a fuck hole, so Van's desire to go slow was a welcome change.

I fondled Van's sac and played with his taint while

leisurely bobbing my head up and down his leaking shaft. Keeping my eyes trained on Van's face, I savored the blissed-out look and the soft grunts he made with each deep thrust of his hips.

"Wanna come," Van growled. "Wanna spill down your throat."

I increased the speed of my movements and teased a finger against his pucker as I imagined burying myself in his ass one day very soon. Van moaned and tensed as his cock throbbed and he spilled his release onto my waiting tongue.

I stood and wrapped my arms around his neck, our spent cocks rubbing together softly. "Thank you, that was amazing."

"You definitely never have to thank me for that," Van said before kissing me deeply and groaning as our flavors mingled.

Once we'd cleaned up, hydrated, and eaten some snacks, we continued on our hike. Walking in nature, enjoying the beauty around us, hand-in-hand with Van, was one of the most enjoyable things I'd done in at least three years.

I couldn't wipe the smile from my face as we met up for fishing with Charlie and Kendall.

"What are you so happy about?" Charlie demanded.

I spread my arms wide. "It's a gorgeous day. We're surrounded by nature. And I'm with friends who love me. What's not to smile about?"

Charlie narrowed his eyes and glanced between Van and me, but turned his attention back to his fishing pole when Kendall elbowed him.

Later that night, as Van and I settled into our sleeping bags, we heard the tell-tale signs of just what Charlie and Kendall were getting up to. We busted out laughing.

Van rolled on top of me. I sighed as he fit perfectly between my legs.

"They're so busy getting their freak on, Charlie won't have a moment to worry about what we're doing," Van murmured against my ear.

We quickly pushed our sleep pants down. With groans and grunts, we began to thrust our cocks together. Van's lips captured my desperate whimpers and we held each other tight as our releases shot hot and thick between us.

After a quick cleanup, Van wrapped me in his arms and pressed a kiss against my temple. "As soon as the business event is done, we tell Charlie. I'm done hiding this from him."

"WHAT DO you mean there's only a king available?" Charlie bit out as we stood in line at the hotel check-in desk. The local business group was meeting in a town next to ours, and we'd decided to make a weekend out of it.

"Sir, you reserved a king room and a double room, but we only have two king rooms available," the flustered clerk explained. "Your event coincides with two other popular events in town this weekend, and we've simply run out of rooms."

Kendall stepped forward. "Two kings are perfectly acceptable. Would you be able to comp us some drinks at the bar due to the mix-up?"

"Of course, that's definitely doable. You'll drink for free this weekend. Please enjoy your stay." The relieved clerk tapped on the keyboard and handed Kendall two envelopes of room keys, along with drink vouchers.

Charlie groused and grumbled as we took the elevator to the tenth floor.

"Dude, lighten up. We're here for one night. Let's try to enjoy it." Van elbowed my brother, but Charlie just grunted.

When Charlie saw the room numbers on the keys, he nearly lost his shit over the fact that the rooms weren't near each other. I, on the other hand, was doing a happy dance and *very* glad I'd packed condoms and lube.

"What time is happy hour?" Van asked.

"Drinks and appetizers in the bar at three. Dinner is at five," Kendall explained as she read from the weekend's itinerary. "Then the main gathering is after dinner. Tonight is the big event. Tomorrow is just brunch after checkout and a brief business meeting."

Van checked his phone as the elevator doors opened. "It's only ten. What are you guys doing until three?"

I wanted to protest and tell him it didn't matter what *they* were doing until three, because I knew what I wanted *us* doing until then.

"We're going to the mall. They've got a scrub shop I want to check out and Charlie wants to take a look at possible locations for expansion." Kendall rolled her suitcase down the hall as we scanned room numbers. "Oh, this is us." She handed Van the other key and half of the drink vouchers. "Honestly, we'll probably come back here and relax. I could do with a nap before everything gets started. And I'll need time to shower and do my hair and makeup."

I glanced at the key in Van's hand and checked the sign on the wall. "Oh, I think we're back the other way."

"I think Sky and I are going to check out the local elementary and some of the shops in Old Towne. Then naps for sure." Van ran a hand over his short dark-blond hair. "Hey, um, probably better let you in on a little plan Sky's helping me with."

Charlie's hackles went up and he narrowed his eyes.

"You know that guy, Topher? He and his mother own the car dealership?" Van asked.

Charlie nodded with a scowl.

Kendall grimaced. "The creepy one with the overbearing mother who is always trying to hook you two up?"

"That's the one. Well, I asked Sky if he'd pretend to be my boyfriend for the weekend to get Topher and Pam off my back." Van took my hand and I couldn't help but chuckle. "So, if you see us being all cozy this weekend, don't freak out."

Charlie gritted his teeth so hard I could almost hear them grinding. "Do you think that's smart?"

"If it gets Pam to back off and Topher to stop eye-fucking me, it's a smart move," Van said.

"I'm not sure it will corral the eye-fucking, but maybe she'll at least give up the dating idea." I shrugged, wanting to bring Van's hand to my mouth and kiss it.

"So, it's all a show? You two are just faking it? It's not real?" Charlie demanded.

Van turned us slightly as if to head down the hall. "If it gets that creep and his mommy to back off, I'm all for it." He pulled me down the hallway as Charlie sputtered and Kendall pushed him into their room.

Once Van unlocked our room, I let out a huge breath I hadn't realized I was holding. "Whoa, so that got a little tense. Do you think he suspects?"

Van dropped his bags and wrapped me in his arms, his chest warm against my back. "He's suspected since your first night here; he's kinda paranoid about the whole thing."

"You didn't actually answer him. I'm sure that's eating at him." I smiled a bit as I took in the gorgeous room and the huge bed.

"I wasn't going to straight-up lie to his face. Once this weekend is over, we're telling him we're together. I didn't want the lie hanging over us." Van shrugged. "I simply evaded."

"Charlie is smart. He knows what you did." I wasn't *scared* of my brother finding out Van and I were together. But I did hate the thought of upsetting him when he'd been so good to me.

"It will all work out. Let's go grab an early, light lunch and check out the school in case you end up with a job here," Van suggested.

It wasn't my ideal location, but I wouldn't turn down a job in a neighboring town.

We each took a moment to freshen up before grabbing our phones and the room key. Van took my hand as we headed down the hallway toward the elevator. Right before we turned the corner, Van drew to a stop and held a finger to his lips as he nodded his head in the direction of the elevators.

"Charlie, they are grown men. If they want to fuck each other's brains out, that's up to them. You have no right to dictate who Van or Sky hook up with or like," Kendall spoke in hushed tones, but not so low we couldn't hear her.

"One or both of them is going to get hurt," Charlie grumbled. "And then I'll be in the middle and have to pick sides. All of this could have been avoided if they'd just listened to me and stayed away from each other." There was a repeated tapping as if he was pressing the down button over and over. "Where the hell is the elevator?"

"Have you even noticed how amazingly happy they both seem lately? Sky looked scared and exhausted—like life-exhausted—when he showed up. He's positively glowing now. The way the two of them look at each other? The happiness just rolls off of them. How can you not see that? Or how can you see it and not be ecstatic for them?" Kendall implored.

There was a long pause.

"What? Tell me. The *real* reason you don't want them together."

"I really am worried it will crash and burn and I'll be stuck in the middle of two heartbroken people," Charlie mumbled.

Van and I took slight steps forward as we strained to hear his words.

"But?" Kendall prodded.

"What if they get together and I lose them? I can't lose my brother and my best friend."

"What do you mean?"

"They get together, fall in love, go off to live their dreams and leave me behind," Charlie muttered. "I know I sound like a big baby even saying that."

My heart caught in my throat and Van squeezed my hand.

"Charlie, I'm going to ignore the implication that being left behind with *me* wouldn't be enough," Kendall teased, "but there's no way in this world that Van or Sky would ever leave you. They both love you. Why not stop worrying about the negative that *might* happen, and focus on the positive that seems to very much be happening? Don't you want your best friend and brother to find happiness?"

The elevator chimed.

"Yeah, just didn't ever think it would be *together*," Charlie groused as they walked through the doors.

Once the car had made its descent, Van and I made our way around the corner in a daze.

"Wow, so he's scared he'll lose us?" I truly hadn't seen that one coming.

"Sounds like it. Really sort of sucks he'd keep the real reason from us. Why bluster and go on and on about not wanting to see us hurt when, in truth, he's just worried he'll lose us?" Van huffed. "I love him, but he's frustrating the hell out of me."

I shook my head. "No, I think he legit does worry about us hurting each other and him getting stuck in the middle.

But a bit deeper, below that basic fear, is the worry he'll lose us. I think he loves being a group of four, so thinking about us becoming our own little couple probably has him freaking out. You know Charlie doesn't like when things go off-script."

Van ran a hand over his face. "We'll still be a group of four." He pushed me into the blessedly empty elevator. "It's just we'll be two couples instead of a couple and two friends. If he's getting to be in love with and sleep with Kendall, I think it's only fair I get to be in love with and sleep with you." He pressed me against the mirrored wall and captured my mouth in a searing kiss.

"Speaking of sleeping with," I murmured against his lips.

We quickly broke apart when the elevator chimed and stopped at floor three.

Van winked at me in the mirror and my face flushed.

Once we were outside on the sidewalk, I continued. "Since we have that nice, big bed and Charlie is waaay down the hall, I thought maybe we could take advantage of the alone time?"

Van bumped his hip against mine. "What exactly are you saying, Mr. Byrd?"

"I'm saying that I brought lube and condoms and I think we should use them tonight," I answered in a breathless rush.

"A plan I can totally get behind. But, I feel like we should build up to it with a little playtime beforehand." He waggled his brows.

"I'm down. Let's eat, check the school, and then get our asses back to the room—I can shop another time; it's not like I have a bunch of money to spend anyway. We have several hours for playtime, sleep, and showers. Then later tonight, you're all mine."

Van leaned close and whispered in my ear, "Can't wait to take that gorgeous cock of yours. Gonna feel so good."

I nearly swallowed my tongue as I shivered at his words. "So, you want to bottom? For real or just because you think I'm like damaged goods?

"Don't get me wrong, I have every intention of burying my cock in your ass, but I'd like to start with me taking you." Van took hold of my elbow and gave it a light squeeze. "I wasn't lying when I said I'd happily bottom full-time if that's what you need."

"Do we even need to get lunch? Is the event all that important? Let's just stay in the room until we have to leave tomorrow." My cheeks were hot and my cock wanted nothing to do with menial tasks like food and business events.

Van laughed. "We need food to fuel up. And we have to be seen together so Topher gets off my back."

I made my voice deep and gruff. "Yeah, 'cause I'm the only one who's going to be on your back." I laughed at myself. I definitely didn't pull off butch very well.

"On me, in me, over me, under me," Van murmured. "I don't care the position, as long as we're together."

"Awww, such a sweetheart. Who knew you were such a romantic?" My heart seriously did flip-flops.

Van laughed. "Not until you." He bumped my hip and then opened the door for me.

We had a nice lunch, took a quick drive past the local elementary school, and then bee-lined it back to the room.

"We've got just over three hours," I said as I glanced at my phone. "Whatever shall we do?"

"Get naked. I wanna feel our skin together," Van whispered gruffly as he peeled his clothes off and tossed them aside.

"Get on the bed," I ordered. "You can watch."

My heart beat an erratic rhythm as Van climbed onto the

middle of the bed, propped himself on the pillows, arms bent behind his head, and his gorgeous cock lying thick against his inner thigh. He licked his lips and gave a devilish smile.

I made quick work of dimming the lights and pulling the blinds to give at least a bit of romantic atmosphere. I checked to be sure the door was locked, and pulled up a playlist on my phone for some background noise.

By the time I returned to the foot of the bed, Van was chuckling. "So much for spontaneous," he teased.

I shrugged. "You'll be glad for my planning when you see my silk panties later tonight," I quipped.

Van groaned. "Oh God, Sky." His dick had hardened even more and now bobbed against his groin. "I can't wait. Wanna kiss your cock through the silk. Will you fuck me with them on? Just pull them down in the front and slide into my ass?"

I shivered and hissed as my cock became painfully hard behind my zipper. "Keep talking like that and we'll *never* get down to the event."

Over the next few minutes, I made a slow show of removing my clothing and teasing Van. His grunts and groans and leaking dick were enough to spur me on and I loved every second of it. I was no longer just a hole—no longer someone's property—and it was a heady feeling.

"Come over here and fuck me," Van demanded.

"What happened to playing around and leading up to that later tonight," I teased as I crawled onto the bed, my throbbing cock swaying heavily.

"It was a stupid idea," Van gritted out. "Want you in my ass."

"Slow and steady wins the race; be patient," I murmured as I straddled his legs and brought our bodies flush together.

Van's hands immediately went to my ass and he squeezed my cheeks as he pulled me tightly against him. "Fuuuuck, that's so good," he groaned as our cocks rubbed together.

"Wanna get off just like this. Then we'll shower; I want to tongue fuck your ass before we nap for a bit."

A tingle of pleasure and anticipation shot through my body as I continued to thrust my hips against his, our precum-slick cocks sliding and rubbing together. Heat surrounded us as our bodies writhed and found a rhythm. "Later, I'll tease your ass with my tongue and fuck you with my finger while I suck your gorgeous cock. Tonight, I'll tuck my panties under my balls, lube my dick, and slide deep into your heat while you moan my name. I'll fuck you hard and slow and my cum will drip onto the silk."

Van gripped my hips and groaned as he continued to rut against me. "Fuck, Sky. Your mouth. So dirty, I love it." He fisted a hand at the back of my head and yanked me close for a searing, soul-deep kiss. "I love you," he whispered against my mouth before devouring it again.

"Mmm, I love you, too," I moaned. "After I come, you'll whimper when I slip from your ass. I'll be worn out from fucking you so hard, but your cock will still be rock-hard." I wrapped my arms around Van's neck and whispered the dirty-talk at his ear. "I'll strip the silk off and spread my legs for you, begging to feel your cock deep inside."

Van groaned. "I'll gather the cum from your panties and smear it against your pretty little pucker before I work my fingers into you, stretching you," he joined in the storytelling. "When you're writhing under me, begging me to fill you, I'll press my swollen cock-head against you. You'll cry out as my cock enters you, but you'll open for me so good. Once I'm balls deep, you'll beg me to move. I'll start slow, but get faster and faster, hitting your spot just right as I fuck into you over and over. You'll clench your ass like a little tease and I'll lose it. I'll come deep inside you, my thick cum pulsing into your heat."

The words we shared, the picture we painted, and the

friction of our cocks was more than enough to send us both over the edge. Van and I came together, our releases meeting and mixing on our bellies as we grunted and groaned and panted each other's name.

Eventually, after what seemed like a year to catch my breath, I chuckled against Van's ear. "Well, I guess we know how tonight's going to play out."

"I'm game if you are," Van growled. "You are so fucking amazing." He ran his hands up and down my back.

"So, before we get too involved in the heat of things tonight. Condoms or no?" I asked.

"That's your call one-hundred percent. I'm perfectly fine with whichever way you're most comfortable." Van's words were a comfort and my heart fell for him even more.

"I think, because we did the screening, I'm down with going without." I rolled from him, wincing as the cool air hit the sticky wetness on my belly. "I know not everyone can or wants to take that route—and with anyone else, I'd be hesitant or downright refuse—but..." I paused.

Van tipped my chin and kissed me softly. "But what?"

"Don't freak out, okay?"

He nodded.

"I kinda feel like you're it for me. Like you're my person."

Van's eyes gleamed and he smiled. "Not going to freak out, as long as you don't. I feel the same. Somehow you went from being my past and my present to being my future," he paused with his forehead pressed to mine, "my forever." His words were thick with emotion. "Maybe it was too quick. Maybe it doesn't make sense to others. But it's what's real and true in my heart." He kissed me, long and deep. "I love you, Sky."

"I love you, too." I wiggled a bit. "But we've got to shower before this gets gross and itchy."

"You go take care of whatever you might need to do for now," Van offered. "I'll join you in a bit."

I reluctantly rolled from the bed, but I appreciated Van giving me a bit of time to prep. Prepping was something Trent always demanded, but acted as if it was a magic wand I could wave and *poof* it was done. *Doesn't work that way, asshole.*

I glanced at the four-pack of enemas I'd thrown in my bag. Presumptuous? Possibly. But I was damn glad I'd thought to toss them in. Once finished, I hollered at him and we spent the next forty-five minutes luxuriating in the fancy shower and eventually filled the tub for a soak.

When we were nearly prunes, Van asked for a bit of privacy and I granted the wish with a kiss as I left the bathroom. The knowledge that he was getting himself ready for me sent shivers through me. I stayed wrapped in my towel and sprawled out on the loveseat while I waited for Van.

When he emerged from the bathroom, he stroked his thickening cock and eyed me. "I thought I was ready for a nap. But I think someone has different plans."

"*Someone* has very good ideas," I murmured as I pushed his naked body onto the bed. "I figure I'll be coming first *tonight*, so it's only fair if you come first today." I grabbed lube from my bag and tossed it on the bed before climbing onto the mattress and kneeling between his legs.

I grabbed a pillow and helped Van prop up his hips for better access. "God, you're gorgeous," I murmured as I bent to nuzzle his balls and skim my lips along his taint.

Van moaned and gripped his cock.

I batted his hand away. "Not yet. That's mine." I blew warm breath against his hole and smiled as he shivered, goosebumps spreading across his skin. I spent several moments licking and tonguing Van's pucker, teasing and twirling my tongue against his most sensitive skin before delving in with slow thrusts.

Van made a whimpery grunting noise. "God, Sky. That's so good. Need more."

I slicked a finger with spit and worked it slowly inside as Van moaned. I added a second finger, stretching his muscle and finding pleasure in the delicious sounds he was making.

"More," Van demanded.

I popped open the lube and spread it on my fingers and his entrance. "Tell me if it's too much."

Van nodded and spread his legs farther apart.

As I slowly worked one, then two, then three fingers into him, I sucked his balls and tongued his taint. Once Van had opened for me completely, I shifted to suck his shaft as I finger-fucked his ass.

Van grunted and ran fingers through my hair.

I knew he didn't want to hurt me or make me think of things from the past, but everything about Van was different —better—so I paused in what I was doing and whispered, "You can pull my hair. Be a little rough."

His eyes glowed with fiery heat and he nodded as I took his hot, salty cock back into my mouth.

I moaned around his shaft when his fist gripped my hair and pulled gently. I continued to thrust my fingers into his ass as he rocked his hips up and gripped my hair.

Spit and pre-cum leaked from my mouth and coated his dick as I took him deep. His body held my fingers tightly as I slid them in and out of his heat.

"Fuck, Sky, I'm gonna come," Van growled.

I increased my speed on his shaft and in his ass and, within seconds, he rewarded me with his thick, hot release exploding on my tongue.

After a few moments, I slid my fingers from his ass and released his spent cock. I grabbed the bath towel Van had left on the floor and wiped the lube from my fingers and the cum from my chin.

With a wicked gleam in his eyes, Van yanked me back onto the bed. "No use in cleaning up when I'm just going to get you dirty again," he whispered gruffly against my ear before kissing the sensitive spot on my neck. "Spread your legs," he ordered.

How did an order like that sound so demeaning and controlling from Trent, yet it was just exciting and sexy coming from Van? *The difference between an abusive relationship and a loving, respectful relationship,* I thought as I moved to take his earlier position on the pillow.

"You okay with this?" Van questioned.

I nodded. "Yeah, definitely. Why?"

"Just seemed like I lost you there for a bit. We don't have to do anything that makes you uncomfortable." Van furrowed his brow.

I shook my head. "Not uncomfortable. I was just thinking how your words and what we're doing are so different than before because there's love and respect between us. That was missing before." I didn't even want to say the bastard's name.

Van leaned in to kiss me. "I love you." A kiss on my nose. "I respect you." A kiss on my forehead. "I cherish you." A kiss to my cheek. "I will always support you." A kiss to my chin. "I value your friendship." A final kiss to my lips.

My eyes stung with tears and I smiled into the kiss. "Such a damn romantic."

Van chuckled as he wiped a tear from the corner of my eye before beginning a long, slow trail of kisses down my body. He stopped to tease my collarbone. He toyed with my nipples as I gasped and writhed beneath him. His tongue dipped into my bellybutton before he made his way to my groin. He placed tiny kisses against the sensitive skin and nuzzled his nose into my dark, trimmed thatch of hair.

By that time, I was ready to hook my hands behind my knees and beg him to just fuck me already, but I controlled the impulse and enjoyed where Van was taking me. When he fondled my balls and pressed his tongue against my hole, I nearly came off the bed.

"Too much?" Van asked.

"No, so good. Haven't had that in over three years. Just forgot how good it is." Trent refused to rim me. Said it made him feel like a girl. Whatever.

Van made a little growly sound—whether out of anger toward Trent or the pleasure he was bringing me, I don't know. But he returned to tonguing my ass and I gripped my cock to stave off a very premature orgasm.

"Stroke yourself," Van demanded as he slipped a finger into my spit-wet hole.

After a few moments, Van lubed his fingers and continued. The second finger brought pressure, the third delivered the stretch and burn I longed for. His fingers found a slow rhythm as he shifted to take my cock in his mouth.

The fullness in my ass and the molten heat around my dick were enough to drive me crazy, but when Van reached his free hand up to tweak my nipples, I knew I wasn't going to last long. The familiar tingle down my spine began and my balls drew up tight. With a slight shift, Van pressed his fingers at a different angle and I cried out as an electric current zinged through me. My orgasm exploded and Van took everything I gave him.

When I finally returned to Earth, Van had wiped himself and me clean and gathered me in his arms.

"I set an alarm. We can sleep for a bit before we need to head downstairs," he whispered against my ear and kissed my temple.

I fell into a deep and comfortable sleep with Van's arms holding me tight.

TWELVE

VAN

"WOULD you stop looking at me like you want to castrate me?" I griped at Charlie.

He narrowed his eyes at Sky's and my joined hands. "Isn't there a better way to do this? Is it really even that important? Just tell Topher and Pam that you're not interested."

"There's nothing wrong with letting someone down easily. Plus, you and Kendall get to drink and have fun. Sky and I should be able to as well." I elbowed him in an attempt to loosen him up.

"I just don't want to find out that you're taking advantage of a situation," Charlie said in a low, threatening whisper.

Kissing Sky's cheek and asking him to go with Kendall for a moment, I cornered Charlie in a hallway near the restrooms. "Do you have something you want to say?"

Charlie's nostrils flared and, for a brief moment, it appeared that he was going to say something—probably something I wasn't going to like. But he gritted his teeth and shook his head. "No, nothing to say."

I poked at his chest. "Good. Because I'm getting really tired of the thinly veiled threats and insinuations that I'm not good enough for Sky." I fought the urge to tell Charlie to fuck off and reveal that Sky and I were dating right then and there. But I wasn't one to cause a scene; the business event was important to Byrd and Badger. And it wasn't fair to Sky to expose our relationship without his input and agreement.

"Would it even matter?" Charlie challenged.

"Would what matter?" I shot back.

"If I had something to say?" His shoulders drooped slightly. "I said my piece before. Would it even matter if I said it again?" Charlie threw a glance over his shoulder to where Kendall and Sky were watching us.

My heart warmed and a smile softened my face as I caught Sky's eye. "I told you before, I'd never hurt him." Unsure of where else to go, I left it there.

"Not even sure that's my biggest worry any longer," Charlie muttered.

When I started to push for more, my best friend shrugged and slapped me on the shoulder.

"Come on, we've got business colleagues to hob-knob with." Charlie turned on his heel and walked away, effectively shutting down any conversation we might have been about to have.

I watched Charlie take Kendall's hand as a worried-looking Sky came my way.

"What was that about?" Sky asked.

"I'm not even sure," I answered quietly as I studied Charlie. "It's almost like he knows, but doesn't want to acknowledge it. Or he knows and is mad we've kept it secret. Or he knows and is afraid of what knowing will do." I huffed and pinched the bridge of my nose. "This is the most unsettled Charlie and I have ever been in our entire friendship."

Sky's face fell. "It's my fault. I'm coming between you." He glanced toward Charlie. "He's done so much for me—

when, in reality, he could have easily thrown me out in the rain—and I've repaid him with sneaking around, secrecy, and lies. I've taken his best friend."

"No," I said a little too forcefully and winced slightly when Sky jumped. "We all three—maybe even Kendall— have made mistakes. It's not like we had any perfect plan to follow. Charlie made it difficult—almost like he forced us into hiding—from the beginning. I don't think we were wrong to hold off until we knew there was something for sure between us." I took Sky's hand. "Maybe we've let the secrecy go a little too far. Maybe Charlie has worked it up in his head to much more of an issue than it should be." I cupped his chin. "But you didn't take me away from him any more than I've taken you away from him. I think that's his biggest fear right now. He's afraid of losing us both. And instead of coming right out and saying it, he's hiding from the truth and building it to a lot more than it needs to be."

"And we're doing the same," Sky added. "What night are you both supposed to be home for dinner?"

I thought about the coming week's schedule. "We should both be home on Tuesday and Wednesday evening—Kendall may be home on Wednesday. They're leaving Friday for a weekend out of town."

"Okay." Sky's eyes gleamed with determination. "We tell him on Wednesday. I want Kendall there to help soften the blow."

"You want Kendall there to help protect us from getting our asses chewed," I teased.

"You're not wrong," Sky quipped with a grin.

"Okay, Wednesday is the plan." I leaned in and kissed Sky's cheek. "Ready to be my fake boyfriend, boyfriend?"

Sky laughed. "It's so strange to go from pretending to *not* be your boyfriend in front of Charlie, to pretending to *be* your boyfriend in front of Topher, while pretending it's fake in front of Charlie."

I grimaced. "Yeah, that needs a flow chart."

"At least while we're in the bar and at dinner, we know we can flirt and touch and be as cozy as we want. Topher will think it's real. Charlie knows it's fake. Supposedly."

"Then let's get drinks and appetizers." I pulled Sky toward the bar.

A few moments later, as we sipped our free drinks and ate some decent appetizers at a high-top table, I heard the sleazy voice I'd been expecting.

"Well, well, well, what do I spy with my little eye?" Topher drawled. "Donovan, dear, if I'd known that you wanted a plus one to our *professional* organization's event, I could have helped you out. You didn't need to go outside of our circle."

I swallowed against a nasty retort and wiped my mouth on a napkin. "Topher," I greeted him and gave a nod over his shoulder to his simmering mother, "Pam. It's nice to see you both. I'd like you to meet my boyfriend, Skyler." Thanks to the nametags we were required to wear, I knew it would only be seconds before Topher glommed onto the fact that Skyler was a Byrd.

"Skyler *Byrd*." Topher gave a creepy smile as he ran his eyes up and down Sky's immaculately dressed body—I wanted to punch him. "Just how does Big Brother Charlie feel about this little love match?"

"Hi, it's nice to meet you," Sky answered as he held out his hand to both Topher and Pam. He completely ignored Topher's question.

They each took it and shook slightly, both with a look of disdain on their pinched and sour faces.

"So, Skyler, *exactly* how are you involved in the business?" Pam asked with a smug smile. She leaned in as if telling a secret. "We don't like to muddy the waters of our organization with non-business-affiliated individuals. I'm sure you understand," she cooed, her scratchy smoker's rasp dripping with artificial sweetener.

"Oh, of course," Sky answered, playing right along. He put his arm around my waist and I immediately wrapped mine around his shoulder. "My brother, Van, and I are in the midst of some exciting expansion plans for Byrd and Badger." He lowered his voice and gave the smarmiest of smarmy smiles—almost even worse than Topher's—as he pretended to let them in on something big. "Not gonna lie. My idea, Charlie's business sense, and Van's experience are working together to build something bigger than any of us could have ever hoped for. Gonna be *huge*."

I nearly laughed out loud at the scene Sky was putting on. I loved it.

"*Van*, huh? I didn't know you went by a nickname," Topher purred, his eyes indicating he didn't want to discuss how Byrd and Badger was expanding and increasing our success. Especially if my boyfriend was involved and getting accolades.

"Only with friends." I kissed the top of Sky's head to hide the smile I was fighting.

Pam intervened with fake interest. "Ah, so just here as business partners then? *Van*, your date will have to excuse you for a dance with Topher after dinner."

I cleared my throat. "It's Donovan. And as I told you, Sky's my boyfriend, not just my date. If we're dancing, it will be with each other."

Topher and Pam both gave identical looks, as if they'd smelled something foul, and glanced around in a way that made me guess they were looking for an escape route from a conversation that didn't go their way.

"Sorry to interrupt," Charlie said with a smile that said he most definitely didn't mind interrupting. "I need to borrow Sky and Van for a bit. Pam, Topher," he greeted the pair, "nice to see you. I hope you're enjoying yourselves."

Charlie ushered us away from the two with a chuckle. "You're welcome. Come on, they're seating for dinner. I want to get four seats together."

I smiled, took Sky's hand, and followed Charlie into the banquet room. I loved that my best friend was so determined to keep our little foursome together. It meant a lot to have a friend who loved his friends and family so much.

My gut churned. Charlie loved Sky and me, yet we'd been lying to him.

"Wednesday," Sky whispered as if reading my thoughts.

I nodded.

We'd clear the air and set things straight Wednesday.

For the time being, I'd enjoy a nice dinner with my friends while looking forward to the after-dinner activities Sky and I had planned. And after Wednesday, we wouldn't have to keep secrets.

SKY PUSHED me against the door the moment it closed behind us.

"That was the most boring event I've ever attended," he murmured into my mouth, "and I've sat through some terrible staff meetings."

"I'd like to say it's usually better when you're not expecting mind-blowing sex after, but it's truly not. We're in the organization for networking, nothing more." I stripped my own shirt and Sky's off before walking him toward the bed. "Give me a few minutes, huh?" I licked at his lips.

Sky nodded.

Within twenty minutes, we'd both taken our turns in the

bathroom, and we found ourselves in a tangle of arms and legs, lips and tongues, our naked skin soft and warm as our bodies writhed together on the sprawling bed.

When Sky rolled me to my back, straddled me with his ass facing me, and bent at the waist to take my cock deep into his hot mouth, I groaned with anticipation of what it would be like to let Sky lead things. He rocked his ass toward me and I licked at his sac as it bumped against my nose.

Sky pulled from my cock with a gasp. "Suck me," he demanded.

I smiled. Sky had been controlled and suppressed for three years. I loved watching him take control and boss me around. Did I look forward to being the one in control at some point? Maybe. Could I be happy with a setup where Sky called all the shots? Definitely.

I fondled his balls as I took his dripping shaft between my lips.

After several moments of deep-throating each other, Sky rolled to the side. "You still want me to fuck you with my silk panties on?" he asked as he ran a thumb over my nipple.

I groaned. "Fuck, yeah." I had no clue why that was such a turn-on for me.

Sky made a show of sliding a pair of red silk panties up his legs and tucking his rock-hard cock in the best he could. He danced around, running palms over his silk-covered dick and ass for a moment while I stroked myself.

"Come over here and fuck me. Pull those panties down under your balls and slide your cock deep in my ass," I demanded. Okay, it was more like *begged*, but whatever.

Sky climbed onto the bed and did as I said. "You want to be on your stomach or back?"

"Wanna watch you," I said as I spread my legs.

He grabbed the lube and spent a few moments stretching me as he sucked my cock before moving up my body to kiss my lips. "You ready for my dick to own your ass?" Sky murmured against my mouth.

I nodded.

"Let me hear the words," Sky whispered.

"Want your dick in me, want you to own my ass," I mumbled.

"This is gonna go very quickly," Sky warned as he took his place between my knees and began to press his swollen head gently against my entrance.

"Doesn't matter. As soon as you come in me, I'm flipping you over and filling you with my cum." I smiled wickedly, gritting my teeth slightly against the sting as Sky's cock began its invasion. "Fuck, that's good," I breathed out.

Sky's cock and balls, propped up by the elastic of his panties, moved forward inch-by-inch as he held my knees open and watched where our bodies joined. "You're so fucking gorgeous. Look at you opening for me, taking me so good," he murmured.

Once he was fully inside, I took a few moments to catch my breath and adjust. "You can move. Wanna feel you."

Sky leaned forward, pressing my legs farther apart, our chests meeting as he kissed my lips. "You're so fucking tight, so hot," he whispered as he began to thrust slow and hard. "Definitely haven't done this in a very long time; not going to last more than a few thrusts," he warned.

"Fuck me, give me all you've got, wanna feel your hot cum in me," I begged.

Panting as he rocked his hips, his balls slapping my ass, Sky buried his face in my neck and made delicious sounds as he fucked into me. "Fuuuuuck," he roared as his cock pulsed and spilled.

My ass clenched around his throbbing cock and I reached between us to squeeze my shaft—I wasn't going to blow until I was buried deep in Sky's body. I let him come down just long enough for his cock to slip from me before I rolled from under him. "My turn," I growled.

Sky let me position him like a rag doll and I yanked his silk panties off before tossing them to the floor. "You okay with this? Or you want to wait?" I didn't want to push.

He nodded with a delirious smile.

I chuckled. "Come on, Sky. Let me hear the words. What do you want?"

"Want you in my ass. Wanna know my cum is dripping from your hole as you pound into me. Wanna feel your hot cock stretch me open," Sky murmured as heavy lashes fluttered around his fiery dark eyes.

I squirted some lube on my cock and spread it against his tight pucker before lining up my dripping head and pressing in slowly.

Sky pulled his legs back and lifted his head to watch my cock disappear into his body. "Fuck, that's so hot," he groaned. "God, feels like you're tearing me apart."

"Is it too much? I can stop." I paused, my cock nearly buried in his heat.

"Fuck, no. Keep going. Want it all," Sky demanded.

"It's a good thing you already got off, because this is going to take like thirty seconds before I blow," I gritted out as I slowly pumped my hips into his exquisitely tight, hot channel. After a few thrusts, I moaned as a wet sensation dripped from my ass. "God, Sky, your cum is leaking from me."

Sky gasped. "Oh, fuck. That's so hot." He pulled me close, his legs spread impossibly wide as our chests came together. "Fuck me, Van. Wanna feel you come in me."

I gathered Sky in my arms and thrust hard and fast into his heat. Within a few moments, I growled out his name and gave one final pump of my hips as my cock exploded and spilled my release in hot pulses.

After a few moments of lazy kisses as we caught our breaths, I pulled from Sky's body with a wince. "You okay? Not too hard?"

Sky shook his head. "That was amazing. Both parts. I know we should shower, but I kinda hate to wash it away."

I kissed him with a smile. "That sort of sounds sweet and sexy, but also sort of gross. Definitely don't want to wash away the feeling of our first time, but I'd rather get the cum rinsed off." I sobered for a moment. "That was a first for me; it was amazing. *You* were amazing." I kissed him again.

We spent the next several hours taking a shower, sleeping, waking for more sex, and then finally crashed until our alarms sounded at nine in the morning. After a quickie, we showered, packed our bags, and met Charlie and Kendall for brunch before the mind-numbingly boring business meeting.

Charlie and Kendall kept throwing glances our way. Charlie's looks were suspicious and angry. Kendall's were teasing and suggestive. I felt totally seen, but I couldn't even care as I wrapped my arm around Sky and kissed his head when Topher and Pam walked into the brunch. Even without the show for the creeps, I would have had a hard time keeping my hands off of Sky. I loved resting my hand on the small of his back as we walked through the door, on his knee and thigh as we sat at the meeting, and brushing our fingers together as we drove home.

We were home and unpacked by Sunday afternoon.

I helped Sky get ready for his week at school.

Kendall went to bed early because she had shifts the next two days.

Charlie went to the bar.

"Wednesday? That's still the plan?" Sky asked.

I nodded. "Wednesday we tell them everything. No more hiding."

THIRTEEN

SKY

THE PLAN WAS to tell Charlie all about us on Wednesday.

Only problem was Charlie came home deathly ill on Monday. Fever, headache, chills, sore throat. He locked himself in his room in hopes of not getting the rest of us sick. Kendall slept on the couch.

Clearly, we couldn't tell him while he was sick.

By the time Charlie was feeling mostly better on Thursday, Kendall was back at work. They were leaving Friday for a weekend away. No way were we dropping our bomb right before their little romantic getaway.

"Okay, we should all be home Sunday night. We'll tell him then," Van offered.

I nodded. "Yeah, sounds good." I wrapped my arms around his waist. "They leave tomorrow before either of us gets home, right?"

Van kissed me, long and slow, before pulling away. "Yeah. I think they're leaving around noon."

"Perfect. We've got all weekend to ourselves. I want to make the most of it," I said.

"I can get behind that plan. What are you thinking?"

"I say we spend most of it in bed. I can't get enough of you," I murmured against his mouth.

"We'll plan for food delivery and copious amounts of sex," Van teased.

"My boyfriend gets me, he really gets me," I teased with a contented sigh. "I love you."

"Love you, too." Van kissed me. "Have a good day at work tomorrow. I'll see you when I get home. Maybe you can be in nothing but silk by the time I get here."

"I can definitely make that happen." I winked and slapped his ass as he gave me one last kiss before heading to his room. One thing I was looking the most forward to was being able to sleep in Van's bed once Charlie knew about us.

I DROPPED my school bag in my room and went straight to the bathroom to shower and prep. The day had been one of those that made me question if teaching was *really* what I wanted to do with the rest of my life. I needed the weekend alone with Van to decompress and relax.

I sent a text to Van telling him he'd find me in his room, then I pulled on a pair of royal blue silk panties with an edge of pinkish purple lace and climbed onto his bed.

Van's bed was comfortable and smelled of him. With a quick glance at the clock, and knowing I had about an hour before he got home, I yanked back the blankets and cuddled in for a nap.

A warm touch ran from my shoulder to my hip as the bed dipped and Van's mouth nibbled at my ear. "I'm going to need you sprawled out in silk, sleeping like an angel in my bed every damn night when I come home," he growled.

"I can probably make that happen," I murmured as I

turned to face him. His naked skin was warm and damp against mine. "Did you shower?"

Van nodded. "You were sleeping so peacefully, I figured I'd let you rest while I got ready."

"Mmm, you smell amazing," I mumbled against his chest and spread my legs so Van could fit his hips against mine.

He wrapped his arms under mine and around my back before capturing my lips with his. The faint flavor of mint and the unique taste of Van filled my senses as his tongue teased mine. "Have I ever told you how fucking sexy you are and how much I love you?" Van studied me with hooded, sexy eyes.

"Maybe, but it will never get old," I answered before kissing him again.

"What do you want?" Van asked several moments later as he pressed kisses against my chest.

My hips rolled and I whimpered as I tried to get more friction against my dick. "Want it hard and slow."

He grunted in response and used his teeth to pull my underwear down. After nuzzling his nose along my thighs and groin, Van moved to suck my cock as he used spit-slick fingers to tease my hole.

"Please," I begged.

Van reached for the lube and covered his shaft before spreading the liquid against my entrance. Pressing his plump head against me, he pressed in slowly. We'd fooled around a bit here and there since getting home from the business event, but it had been a week since I'd taken him and I hissed against the stinging intrusion.

He paused, a look of concern on his face. "You okay?"

I nodded. "Yeah, just go slow."

Van continued to sink into me inch-by-glorious-inch until his balls brushed my ass. "So good," he said in a gruff whisper.

Letting my legs fall open, I reached for Van and pulled him close to my chest. "Hard and slow."

He began an agonizingly slow rhythm of hard thrusts. Each pump of his hips jarred me and sent pleasure zinging through me, and I almost begged him to speed it up. Instead, I wrapped my legs around his waist and let him hold me as he fucked into me while whispering a mix of dirty and loving words at my ear.

"Want you to come with me," Van said on a slow retreat before sliding his throbbing shaft back in hard and deep.

I'd never been able to come while Trent fucked me. I was always too on-guard of what he might do next. And he never cared if I got off or not. But Van's lower abdomen brushed against my cock with each thrust of his hips and I knew I'd be able to orgasm with just a few strokes.

I reached for myself, but Van shifted, rolling to his back and hoisting me to straddle him. "Fuck yourself on me," he demanded as he reached for my cock.

The change in position had me gasping as Van's dick slid even deeper. My leaking cock bobbed heavily and I moaned as Van ran his thumb over my slit.

I leaned forward, my arms braced on the headboard, and Van brought his knees up to support me. I continued the slow pace as I slammed my ass down on Van's cock, whimpering with each press of his head against my prostate.

Van's big hand stroked me with a slow, steady rhythm. "Come for me, Sky. Want you on my skin."

"Gotta go faster," I whimpered. "Pump your cock into me, hard and fast."

Van gripped my hips as I began to jack myself. He pistoned his hips even harder as he picked up the pace. Within moments, my balls tightened and I shot thick ropes of cum onto Van's stomach as he groaned and pumped his release into my ass.

I collapsed onto his chest, not minding the sticky mess between us. Tucking my head under his chin, I smiled and enjoyed the euphoria that washed over me.

"I know we've got all weekend, and I know we can't spend the *whole* time having sex," Van mumbled against the top of my head, "but I wouldn't mind pizza and another round of that before bed."

"Only if I get to top," I answered without even opening my eyes.

"Not a problem," Van said.

We took a couple hours to order pizza, clean up, and eat our dinner while we chatted about Byrd and Badger and school. My eyes were beginning to get heavy, and I knew— even with the nap—that the week was catching up with me.

"I think we better get round two under way before I fall asleep," I joked.

"We don't have to have sex. We can just go to bed." Van wrapped me in his arms and walked me to his room.

"Nope, I'm totally in the mood. Just know that I'll be sleepy sooner rather than later, so we better get a move on." We'd eaten dinner in just our underwear, so I only had to slip mine off before pulling Van's down his legs. "What do you want?"

"Rough," Van answered gruffly. "Wanna choke on your cock. Want you to fuck me so hard I feel it tomorrow."

"Jesus, Van," I groaned.

Van smiled wickedly as he settled himself in the middle of the bed and propped himself against the pillows. "Come here and fuck my face," he demanded.

My cock twitched as I straddled his hips and shimmied my way up to his chest.

Van licked his lips.

I pressed my leaking head against his bottom lip and smeared the pre-cum before smacking my shaft against Van's cheek. "Open for me." His lips stretched around my cock as I fed it to him. "So good," I murmured.

Van's hands took hold of my ass and pulled me forward as if reminding me how he wanted it. Taking hold of the headboard, I lifted my hips and began to snap them in a hard and fast rhythm as I fucked Van's face. Deliciously dirty sounds filled the room and I knew I could have exploded if I wanted to. Van took me deep, the blissed-out look on his face telling me he loved every minute of it.

But I wanted more. I pulled from his mouth and grabbed the lube. Tossing it to the side, I waited for Van to move to his hands and knees. I'd never been allowed to explore this side of myself before. I definitely loved bottoming, but being able to test the waters and experiment with other positions gave me a confidence I didn't even know I had.

Smacking my hand against Van's ass—and smiling when he growled—I spread his cheeks and devoured his hole until he was loose and ready.

"God, Sky. Please, just fuck me," Van begged.

After lubing myself and Van, I slid into his heat and paused for a moment to gather myself.

"Hard and fast," Van reminded me.

I gripped his hips and thrust just like he'd asked me to, but I wanted more. "Lay on your stomach," I demanded.

When Van dropped to the bed, I wrapped my arms under and around his chest and pumped hard and fast into his ass. The full-body contact was just what I needed and I knew I'd hit my release quickly. "Can you come this way?" I asked on a harsh breath against Van's ear as my hips pistoned into him.

"Want your cum in me first, then you can get me off," Van answered, panting.

I pushed up on my arms and watched as my cock slid in and out of Van's perfect ass. Within moments, I tensed and spilled my release with a groan.

When Van's ass had milked me dry, I pulled out and rolled him over. I spread lube into my crack and straddled him. With Van's thick shaft nestled between my ass cheeks, I began to rock my hips, sliding my ass along his cock as Van grunted and groaned beneath me.

"Fuck, Sky, fuck," he bit out.

I shifted to his thighs and took his dick in my hand. After only three strokes, Van came apart in my fist.

"Was that too much?" I asked a few moments later after we'd cleaned up and cuddled back into bed without bothering to put on clothes.

"Fuck, no. It was amazing. I love being able to switch things up with you. Love that there's no *right* or *wrong* in how we chose to love each other." Van kissed the top of my head. "And I will definitely feel it tomorrow. Mission accomplished."

We fell asleep in each other's arms.

"HAVE YOU SEEN SKY?" Charlie demanded as the door to Van's bedroom flew open. "Are you fucking kidding me?!"

Bright light made me wince and told me it was morning.

Van's arm wrapped around me and his hard cock pressed against my naked ass reminded me I was in his bed.

But my head wasn't wrapping around why a seething, snarling Charlie was standing in the doorway of Van's room.

Did we sleep through the weekend?

"Charlie?" Van tightened his arm against me and propped up on an elbow. "Why are you in my room? And why are you home?"

"I'm *home* because Kendall got sick and wanted to come home. I'm in your room because I was worried that Sky wasn't here even though his car was," Charlie growled. "How long were you planning to lie to me?" he demanded.

"Charlie!" a weak and pitiful Kendall yelled from down the hall.

He grimaced and pointed a finger. "Get dressed. We need to talk."

THIRTY MINUTES LATER, Van and I had showered. Charlie had made coffee and tea. Van warmed up some cinnamon roll samples he'd brought home from the bar the day before.

Kendall shuffled to the living room and plopped miserably in the recliner.

"You don't have to be here," I said. "You look like you feel horrible. Don't worry about our sorry asses, we'll figure it out." I felt terrible that she was out of bed and dealing with our shit.

Kendall shook her head. "I took some pain relievers. I'm going to drink some tea, eat a cinnamon roll—because those look amazing—and make sure you three get your heads out of your asses and don't make things worse. Then I'm going to bed."

Charlie brought the coffee carafe and the makings for tea into the living room. Van carried the warm rolls and placed them on the coffee table.

We all sat down and an awkward silence filled the room.

"Charlie, why don't you start," Kendall suggested as she warmed her palms around the mug of coffee.

My brother scowled and said nothing.

"Words, Charlie. How are you feeling?" Kendall nudged his knee with her foot.

With a huff, Charlie began. "I'm pissed. You guys went

against what I specifically asked you *not* to do. And you lied to me. How long did you think you could keep it from me?" Charlie bit out.

"Charlie, you're my best friend and I love you," Van began, "but it wasn't fair of you to demand that Sky and I stay apart."

Charlie grunted.

"No," I interrupted. "The fact that you immediately demanded we stay apart was unfair because you just assumed two gay men would automatically be attracted to each other. When Van and I *did* find ourselves drawn to each other beyond our old friendship, your demand was unfair again; would you really keep your best friend and your brother from being happy even if it means we're together?" I took a deep breath. "I guess I could see it if there was bad blood between you and me—and maybe you're angrier at me than you've ever admitted—but I can't see why you wouldn't want two people you supposedly love *not* to be happy."

Charlie flinched. "I'm not angry at you. I hate that we lost three years because of that asshole, but I'm not mad at you."

"So why wouldn't you want Van and me to be happy?" I pushed.

Charlie sipped his coffee, but didn't speak.

"Look, while you dig deep for that answer, I need you to know a few things," Van cut in. "Sky and I didn't get into this relationship lightly. It wasn't just to piss you off or hurt you. We actually hesitated for a bit because we didn't want to upset you."

My brother listened as he chewed his cinnamon roll slowly.

"At first, we thought there was no reason to even tell you we were attracted to each other if it wasn't going to go anywhere," Van explained as he took my hand.

Charlie stared at our joined hands as if his brain was

about to short-circuit. Like he couldn't wrap his head around Van and me together.

"But when we realized that our past and our present had collided and brought us to something that neither of us have had before—a real relationship built on love and respect—we opted to accept our happiness even if it meant going against what you wanted." Van ran his thumb over my knuckles.

"*Love?*" Charlie scoffed. "You *love* each other? Little fast don't you think? Sky, you're fresh out of a bad situation. Van, you've run through more casual hook-ups than I can count. How can you guys claim you love each other after such a short amount of time?"

"*Because* of what I'm fresh out of, I recognize how different what I have with Van is," I answered quietly. "It may not make sense, but I've loved Van in one way or another since I was a child. What we've found in each other came so naturally—honestly, we didn't even see it coming—and I hate to think you're angry, but I'm not going to throw away love and happiness because you're bent out of shape." I swallowed thickly, afraid of how the situation was going to play out.

"Charlie, we've been together since that first night that was supposed to be just a hook-up," Kendall chimed in softly. "How quickly did we know we wanted to be together forever?"

He shot her a look, but his face softened a fraction. "How do you know you're not just both on the rebound or settling?"

"So, someone who would want to be with either of us would be *settling*?" Van asked with a tinge of anger. "That's a bunch of bullshit, Charlie. I love Sky with my entire being. I've loved him since we were little. That love moved so easily from friendship to a romantic love, I didn't even realize it was happening. I may not be the best catch, but I love him and I'd never let him just *settle* if I wasn't one hundred percent sure that we're good for each other."

"Charlie, I'm tired. I want to sleep. I think you need to tell them what you're really afraid of and then take me to bed," Kendall said as she finished her breakfast and coffee.

Charlie sighed and closed his eyes. "Let's just get you to bed," he offered.

"No, Charlie. Words. Truth. This friendship is based on love and honesty and respect. We can't all grow together if we don't communicate." Kendall gave Charlie a look and took his hand.

"I don't even know how to explain it. I love you both. I want you both in my life. But seeing you together makes me worry that you'll leave me. I'll lose my brother all over again *and* my best friend because you've found each other." Charlie's words poured from him and he leaned forward on his knees to hold his head in his hands.

Van and I knew this was Charlie's fear, but it helped to hear it directly from him.

"Charlie, you're my best friend. We made it through high school, me leaving the country, me coming out to you, and building a business together. Surely you don't think I'd leave you—and take your only brother away from you—just because Sky and I unexpectedly fell in love?" Van frowned. "You, Sky, Kendall, your parents, you're the only family I have. I love you all. Sky and I aren't going anywhere."

I nodded, tears stinging my eyes. "I guess I can see if you and Kendall one day want a house by yourselves—or maybe Van and I might want our own place—but I plan on being a part of Byrd and Badger as well as a beloved local Kindergarten teacher." I winked with a smile. "I have no plans to leave this area. Van is here. You and Kendall are here. Mom and Dad are here." I shrugged. "I kinda thought the four of us could build a life here."

Charlie sniffed and cleared his throat. "Sorry, I guess I let my insecurities get the best of me. And I'm sorry for making it seem like I think you two aren't good for each other. It may take me a bit of time to get used to it, but I love you both and if you're happy together, then I'll be happy for you." He sniffed again, but tried to hide it behind a scowl. "But I swear to God, if either of you hurt the other…"

"They're big boys. You don't have to clean up their messes," Kendall interrupted. "Now, I need to go to bed." She turned to look at me and Van. "I'm sorry we messed up your weekend alone. Since everything is out in the open now, don't think you have to hide or keep secrets. Maybe we should all invest in earplugs."

"Ewww, no. I do *not* want to think of my brother and best friend having sex. I'm working at being okay with this, but I'm not completely there yet." Charlie grimaced and took Kendall's hand.

"Then you *really* should get some earplugs," Van teased, "because neither of us are very good at keeping quiet. Surprised we didn't get complaints at the hotel."

Charlie growled. "La-la-la, I'm not listening to you," he chanted as he and Kendall headed toward their bedroom.

"Hey, Charlie?" I called out.

"What?" he shot back.

"Don't worry about getting me a bed or changing the office to my bedroom. I'll be in Van's bed from now on," I called out. "Every night. Every morning. Doing crazy dirty things with him."

"Fuck you both!" Charlie called out, but I heard the laughter in his voice.

I smiled and leaned into Van's arm. "Okay, on a scale of disaster to amazing, that definitely wasn't horrible."

"Agreed." Van kissed the top of my head. "I think Kendall

is a lifesaver. She's his balance. We likely would have been closer to disaster without her input and calming presence."

"I *am* sorry we lied to him," I muttered.

"Same. He kinda put us in a bad situation, but we should have just told him to fuck off with his demands and been honest from the beginning." Van put his arm around me and pulled me to lay down on the couch alongside him.

"Lesson learned," I whispered as I cuddled into his chest. "Those cinnamon rolls were amazing. Are we selling them at breakfast?"

Van nodded. "I think so. Tomorrow we can taste the tea samples to see which we want to carry. I think Charlie and I have decided on the coffee. We've got some breakfast sandwich choices to make, too."

"As part of the team, I'll totally volunteer to help with those decisions," I teased.

"Do you really think Charlie is okay with us?" Van asked a few moments later.

"I think he's really going to do his best to be okay with us. I mean, he's not having trouble with us being gay and together. I think he's more envious of the closeness of our relationship."

Van snorted. "I guarantee Charlie isn't jealous of our sex life."

"No, not the sex." I elbowed him. "No matter how close he and I are because we're brothers, and no matter how close you and he are because of a lifetime of friendship, he'll never have with us what you and I have together. I kinda get it. Just like you'll never have with either of us what Charlie and I have because we're brothers. And I'll never have what you two have as best friends. When you love someone as much as the three of us love each other, it can sometimes be hard to see the other person have something with someone else." I shrugged. "I don't know if that even makes sense. I think we're lucky he has Kendall so he doesn't feel completely left out."

"Why does he have such a problem with our sex life?" Van murmured.

"Do *you* want to think about Charlie's dick? Or him and Kendall getting it on?" I asked.

Van shivered. "Okay, point made."

I chuckled.

We cuddled quietly for several moments before Van broke the silence. "Hey, I *may* have made an inquiry and possible contact for that threesome we were talking about," he whispered against my ear.

My eyes shot open and my dick stirred. "For real?"

"Mmhm," Van hummed. "Let me get a little bit more information and then we can discuss it. If you're down with the situation, we'll see if the third is open to what we're wanting. Don't want to rush it. We'll take our time and make sure everyone is onboard. But, as long as you're still interested, I'll keep trying to make it happen."

"I'm definitely still interested." I rocked my hips against Van's. "But, until we can make that happen, there's something else I'm *very* interested in."

We spent the rest of the weekend naked in bed. Charlie grumbled each time he left a delivery bag of food outside our door, but by Sunday night, the three of us sat in the kitchen sampling tea and breakfast sandwiches and laughing. I had my boyfriend—my past, my present, and my future—*and* my brother in my life. With a teaching job, Kendall, my parents, and Byrd and Badger, my life had definitely taken a turn for the better. No, not *better*. The *best*.

FOURTEEN

VAN

Two months later

"You ready?" I asked Sky as we neared the patio area of Byrd and Badger.

Our relationship was perfect—okay, no relationship is *perfect*, but we were madly in love and doing great—and we'd finally pinned down a time to make the threesome happen.

"Yeah, kinda nervous, but mostly excited." Sky smiled and took my hand. "I'm glad we're starting out this way. I feel comfortable knowing we can call it off easily if things don't feel right."

I gave his hand a squeeze. Before Sky expressed his interest in a threesome, I would have been down for a quickie with two guys, but I never would have thought I'd be willing to share my *boyfriend* with another man. Now though? Knowing how turned on Sky was about the prospect had me looking forward to the possibility just as much as him.

Matt was a Byrd and Badger employee which probably was a very bad idea. However, Matt was moving to California in a few short weeks. So, yeah. The idea wasn't actually that bad.

"What if he doesn't like me?" Sky whispered as we wound through the crowded patio.

"Not possible. Have you *seen* you?" I kissed the side of his head and raised an arm in greeting when I saw Matt at a far corner table.

"Oh my God, he's hot," Sky muttered.

"Told you. I worked hard at making this work out. I wasn't just going to pick *any* guy who was willing. Matt is attractive, nice, hardworking, and discreet. He had no issue with providing me with a clear screening report." I'd shared ours with Matt as well. We were using condoms with him, but clear tests were important to all three of us. "And if things get weird, he's moving in a couple weeks."

"Hi," Matt stood to greet us with handshakes. "Nice to meet you," he said to Sky with a wink. The way he looked Sky up and down and bit his lip probably would have made me jealous at any other time. But knowing he was attracted to my boyfriend and all the things we'd maybe be doing in just a few short hours had me glad my shirt wasn't tucked in and could hopefully hide the way my dick plumped at the thought.

"Are any of you on the clock?" Charlie asked as he delivered drinks to a nearby table.

We all laughed and told him no.

"Well, we're swamped so get your own drinks and food. I'm not waiting on you," he groused, but winked and laughed as he rushed away.

Charlie had adjusted to Sky and me being together. I think he needed to see that we could love each other without pulling away from him. The four of us were happy and settling in nicely. Sky and Kendall had begun bonding over wine and wedding plans.

Charlie and Kendall's wedding plans.

I definitely wanted to marry Skyler. But we needed some

more time to just be a couple before rushing into marriage. And neither of us wanted to steal the spotlight from Charlie and Kendall.

Sky had graduated from college and gotten his teaching license. None of that had been in question—we all knew he'd pass with flying colors. But his biggest concern was getting a job in a grade he wanted *and* at a school in town, or at least nearby. His host teacher had given him a great recommendation, and the principal at the local elementary where Sky did his student teaching loved him. So, it was a dream come true when Sky landed a Kindergarten position at Oakhurst Elementary just down the road from our house. He had a summer of professional development and planning and purchasing items for his classroom to look forward to—and I planned to help him with every single bit of it if I could.

But he wanted to take a break from all things school for a little bit. Which was why the timing with Matt was perfect for everyone involved.

"So, we were thinking dinner and then heading to your place if we're all feeling it," I said quietly. "No alcohol here. Only a couple drinks or shots at yours if desired."

"We don't want to be sloshed," Sky cut in with a soft smile.

"Agreed. If dinner goes well, we can each take a bit of time to ourselves and then meet up at my apartment. I've got it to myself for the week. The new guy moves in next week, but for now it's completely empty." Matt sipped his water and somehow made it look sexy.

Once we were ready for food, I went to the kitchen to put in our orders and Matt went to pick them up a bit later. I noticed with a smirk that we'd all kept our meals pretty light. Either from nerves or anticipation of later or both.

As we ate, we fell into an easy conversation and the flirt level was high. I loved watching Sky get flirty—the blush on his cheeks and the heat in his eyes were adorable, and he somehow managed to flirt with Matt while still making me feel like the very center of his world.

"I know we've discussed it some, but maybe we should talk about our wants and our limits," I suggested quietly as I took a bite of my turkey wrap.

"I only top," Matt said in a low voice. "Van didn't think that would be a problem?" he asked Sky.

"No, that's okay. If we were to ever do this again, I'd maybe be interested in changing it up, but this time, I'd like to be in the middle." He turned to me. "Are you okay with bottoming for me if I'm taking Matt?"

I swallowed and nodded. "Yep." That was about the only word I could get out around my suddenly thick tongue.

"I always thought no kissing, but I'm open to it if it feels right," Sky said and licked his lips. I had a feeling it would feel very right.

"Condoms are a must," Matt added. "I'll rim either of you if you want, but I don't want it done to me."

"Is this a one-and-done or are multiple times through the night an option?" I asked.

"I'm open for second and third rounds if you boys are," Matt answered with a smirk.

"And we're clear this is sex only," Sky asked. "Van and I are in a committed relationship. We're not looking for a third outside of just sex."

"That's the only way I'd do it. I'm moving, plus I'm not looking to be a third or even looking for a relationship right now." Matt nodded as he wiped his mouth and placed the napkin over his half-empty plate. "What do you guys think? Is this going to happen?"

I glanced at Sky and he smiled with a sexy, wicked gleam in his eyes.

"Give us your address," I said. "We'll run home and get ready. Be there in under an hour?"

Matt and I had exchanged numbers earlier and he texted me his address before we paid for our food and headed out with quick waves to Charlie.

"Oh my God," Sky whispered giddily. "Can you imagine if Charlie had any idea what was going on right now?" He giggled.

"Pretty sure that would bring on a nuclear meltdown."

We rushed home and took turns in the bathroom before meeting in our bedroom to make out and get dressed. As my hands ran down over Sky's ass, a thought hit me. "Are you wearing your silk?" The idea felt a little funny in my gut, but I'd accept whatever Sky wanted to do.

He rolled his hips gently, our semi-hard cocks rubbing together softly. "I will if you want me to, but I kinda wanted to keep the silk between just us."

I leaned in and devoured his mouth until we were both moaning and rocking our hips together. "I like that. I don't mind giving you this; I'm looking forward to it. But seeing you in silk is something I want to keep for just my eyes."

Sky nodded. "I love you. Nothing that happens tonight changes that. Thank you for giving me this."

I kissed him soundly. "I love you. You're going to look so damn sexy with his cock in your ass," I growled and felt the heat of the words straight to my groin.

"Fuck, Van," Sky whimpered. "Do you want him to fuck you?"

"Maybe if he ever comes back to visit and we rendezvous. But tonight is about you and what you want. Plus, how can I complain? I'll be getting pounded by you while he's railing your ass. Pretty sure I'll be loving it no matter how it plays out."

"There's always an option of round two," Sky suggested with a kiss to my chin.

We dressed quickly and threw clothes, toothbrushes, and supplies into a bag in case we decided to sleep over. Honestly, I was open to whatever Sky wanted to do.

We arrived at Matt's place in just under an hour.

"Here, I'll throw that in my room," Matt said as he took the bag. "You guys want a drink?" His dark hair was wet and he'd only slipped on a pair of lounge pants after his shower. His broad shoulders, rippled abs, and thick torso were lickable and I suddenly wanted to see Sky and Matt touching.

"Couple shots?" I suggested.

Sky nodded and licked his lips as he watched Matt return and set up six shot glasses.

"Fireball?" Matt asked. "Or," he rummaged in the liquor cabinet, "I've got tequila or vodka."

"Fireball is fine," Sky answered for both of us.

I seriously didn't give a fuck what I was drinking at that moment.

"To a fun, sexy time," Matt toasted and we each took our two shots back-to-back.

"Oh, it burns," Sky gasped.

Matt turned heavy eyes toward Sky and smirked as I plastered my chest to Sky's back.

I slid Sky's shirt over his head and ran my hands over his nipples. "You like the burn," I teased as I dipped my head to kiss his neck. I smiled against his skin when he shivered.

Matt took a step forward and I pressed Sky closer, like he was the filling of our little body sandwich.

"Like the burn, huh?" Matt placed his hands on mine and helped me tweak Sky's nipples. "You'll love my cock then," he whispered at Sky's ear.

"Oh, fuck," Sky panted. He snaked his arms around Matt's waist.

Matt's arms came around Sky and me and he ran his hands up and down my back.

I shoved Matt's and Sky's waistbands down quickly before taking their cocks in my fist and stroking.

Sky's head fell back against my chest and Matt's mouth followed with kisses along Sky's jaw. When Matt's mouth paused at Sky's lips, I increased my strokes and whispered, "Do you want to kiss him?"

Sky whimpered a breathy, "Yes," and Matt devoured Sky's mouth.

"Fuck, that's so hot," I growled as I pressed my rock-hard cock against Sky's ass.

Sky broke the kiss. "Kiss him," he demanded.

Matt's lips stopped just shy of touching mine. I appreciated the moment to grant consent. I nodded and met his mouth. Matt was a good kisser. It wasn't as earth-shattering as kissing Sky—there was no emotional connection—but his mouth on mine felt good.

"Turn around," Matt ordered Sky.

Sky turned in my arms and immediately wrapped his arms around my neck like a puzzle piece clicking into place. "Hi," he whispered against my lips.

"Kiss him," Matt said as he repeated my action by pulling my pants down and stroking my and Sky's cocks.

Sky's tongue plunged into my mouth and I moaned as I ran my hands down Matt's back to grip his ass.

"Bedroom?" Matt suggested.

We made our way to Matt's bedroom and the moment was broken slightly as the reality of what was about to happen came crashing through the lust-filled haze.

"What do you want?" Matt asked Sky. I liked that he knew this was Sky's show.

Sky's face flushed and I knew his mind had gone a bit kinky.

"Tell us, Sky," I whispered as I slipped my pants and underwear off.

Matt followed suit and we stood there, cocks bobbing, watching Sky blush and stumble around his answer.

"Want you both," Sky said with a furious blush.

"You wanna lay back on that bed, spread your legs, and let us take turns sliding our cocks in your pretty little hole," Matt supplied.

"Fuck," I growled as Sky nodded and whispered, "Yes, fuck yes."

"Take them off," Matt ordered.

Sky shimmied out of his pants.

Matt rummaged through his side table drawer and came up with lube and a whole strip of condoms. "You good with these?"

I nodded and took a condom from him. "Lie down," I told Sky. My cock twitched at how fast he scrambled to the edge of the bed and spread his legs.

Matt stood next to me and we both dropped to our knees at the same time.

Sky gasped and nearly came off the bed when both my and Matt's tongue touched his entrance. "Don't touch yourself," I demanded. "We're going to work you open and fuck you. Don't want you coming yet."

Matt and I spent several moments rimming Sky's ass, breaking every so often to kiss each other. Skyler seesawed between throwing his head back on the bed with a grunty, whimpering sound and propping himself on his elbows to watch Matt and me eat his ass and make out.

"Fuck, wanna feel you," Sky begged.

"You wanna go first?" Matt asked.

I took Matt's dick in my fist and kissed him as I stroked his thick shaft. "Yeah, he's going to need a bit of prep to take this monster."

Matt chuckled as he took hold of my hips and guided me to stand between Sky's spread legs. I grunted as Matt fisted my cock and rolled a condom down my length. He pumped lube into his hand and slicked me before teasing a slippery finger into Sky's tongue-fucked hole.

Sky writhed as Matt finger-fucked him. "Please," Sky begged.

Matt took my cock in his hand and pressed my head against Sky's pucker. "Fuuuuck," Matt growled. "Look at how your boy opens for you."

I grunted and took in the scene. The man I loved was spread before me, taking me in the most intimate of ways, while Matt fed my shaft into Sky's greedy hole. Sensation overload was an understatement.

Matt stood behind me, plastered to my back, and reached around to grip Sky's hips as he fell into my thrusting rhythm. Matt's hard length pressed against my ass. Right when I nearly forgot Matt was there and focused only on Sky, Matt pulled me away.

"My turn," he said as he rolled a condom on and slid into Sky's stretched hole.

Sky gasped at the thicker invasion, but pulled his legs higher and made the sexiest moaning sounds each time Matt's thick cock slammed into him.

Matt glanced my way and nodded toward where he and Sky were joined. "Back and forth, take turns, ruin that pretty little hole."

I leaned onto the bed. "You okay with us taking turns?"

Sky whispered yes and kissed me desperately.

Matt and I took the next few minutes taking turns sliding our dicks in and out of Sky's gaping hole.

"Stop," Sky cried. "I'm gonna come. Gotta stop."

Glad for the break—I was within seconds of blowing my load—I took a moment to catch my breath and calm my dick. Every time I watched Sky take Matt's cock, I nearly exploded.

"Van, you want to be on your stomach or back?" Sky asked as he rolled to grab a condom and sheath his throbbing cock.

In answer, I stripped off the condom I'd been wearing and bent over the edge of the bed with my legs spread.

"Mmm," Matt groaned as he ran a finger over my hole.

Before I knew what was happening, Matt and Sky were on their knees, their tongues dueling as they rimmed me. "Fuuuuck," I cried out. "Need a cock in me, now," I begged. I didn't care who fucked me, but my ass ached with wanting to be filled.

Sky pumped lube along his shaft and pressed his head against me. I moaned as he breached my entrance. He leaned forward and pressed his chest against my back. "I'm going to tell you how it feels when Matt's fat cock is deep in my ass. Every time he pumps into me, I'll be fucking into you."

I turned my head for an awkward and messy kiss with Sky. "Get in his ass," I ordered Matt when Sky and I parted.

I felt Matt's presence when Sky shuddered and put more weight on my back. "Tell me," I murmured to Sky.

"He's spreading lube and fingering my hole," Sky whispered. "Now he's pressing his thick head against me. Fuuuuck," Sky groaned, "he's so damn big."

"You okay?" Matt asked.

"Yeah, it's good." Sky wrapped his arms under my chest. "You good?"

I nodded. "Someone needs to move," I begged.

Matt began to thrust and Sky whimpered.

"Sensation overload," Sky muttered. "Fuck, your ass is so hot and tight, but my ass is so full and he's hitting me just right. It's so fucking good," he panted.

Each and every time Matt thrust into Sky, a jolt of electric current traveled through me as Sky's dick brushed my prostate. "I'm not going to last very long," I warned.

"Jack yourself," Matt ordered me as he began to pound into Sky.

I reached between my body and the bed and took my throbbing cock in my hand. Within three or four strokes, I cried out and spilled over my fist as my entire body shuddered under the weight of Sky and Matt.

"You close?" Matt asked Sky.

Sky mumbled something unintelligible, but I knew he wasn't going to last very long. Matt pumped his hips harder and faster. Sky tensed and his cock began to pulse in my ass just as Matt slammed into him and came with a low groan.

Holy.

Fucking.

Shit.

We lay in a panting pile for a few moments.

"That was fucking amazing," Sky whispered. "Right?" his voice held just a hint of worry.

"Fucking amazing," I agreed.

"I've only ever done that one other time," Matt said, "but this was hands down the best sex I've ever had."

The weight on my back lessened as Matt and Sky both moved.

I felt empty and alone.

Matt shuffled to the bathroom. I heard him toss the condom, and he returned with a washcloth for both of us. "I'm completely down with resting and doing that again if you're interested." Matt cleaned his soft cock and tossed the cloth to the floor.

Sky disappeared just long enough to throw away the condom. He bit his lip and nodded when he returned. "I think we can stay."

The three of us piled into Matt's bed and ended up in

some sort of oddly comfortable tangle of arms and legs. We slept for several hours, waking as sunlight began to filter into the room.

Our second round was slower, but no less hot as we took each other on our sides. I found myself in the middle, impaled on Matt's cock and buried in Sky's ass. Both felt glorious, but being in Sky was the definition of *good* and *right*. Every time my dick slid into Sky, it was like coming home. I reached around and stroked his leaking cock as I whispered how much I loved him against his ear. Matt thrust hard and deep into my ass and kissed my neck. Our releases shattered through us almost simultaneously and we stayed in a tangled mess for several moments while coming back to earth.

Matt offered us the spare bathroom while he took the master. Sky and I washed the night away and embraced under the spray of warm water.

"I need you," Sky whimpered against my mouth. "Just you, bare inside me."

I growled and lifted him so his legs wrapped around my waist. Shower sex wasn't nearly as glamorous as it appeared in porn, but I pushed gently into Sky's ass. "Are you too sore?" I rocked my hips slowly.

"No, need to feel you come in me," he begged before devouring my mouth.

"Are you okay?" I worried the night before was becoming a regret.

"Last night was amazing, but I need to know you're here. Need you to make me yours," he muttered between the sexy little sounds he made with every thrust. "Love you so much, Van."

"Love you," I grunted. "Gonna fill you with my cum," I promised. "Then I'll suck your cock until your knees buckle."

And that's exactly what I did.

"YOU DAMN SON OF A BITCH," Charlie roared as he barreled into the kitchen with his fist drawn back as if he planned to punch me.

"Whoa," Sky yelled and grabbed Charlie's arm. "What the fuck, Charlie?"

"And what did my mom ever do to you? I didn't even know her," I tried to joke, but anger shot from Charlie's eyes.

"I won't stand by and let you hurt him," Charlie seethed.

"What the actual fuck are you talking about?" I held my hands up.

"I always thought you were brilliant, but I guess you're not smart enough to keep your hook-up from talking at work," Charlie bit out.

My eyes strayed to Skyler for the briefest of moments before I cocked my head at Charlie. "You're going to have to be more specific because I'm completely lost. The only hooking up I've been doing is with Sky."

"Bullshit," Charlie growled. "I heard you talking to Matt."

I couldn't risk a look at Sky, so I narrowed my eyes at my best friend. "When did you hear Matt and me talking?" *Oh shit.*

"Today! You went to the backroom and were gone forever so I stopped to check on you before I went to my office. Don't even try to deny it. I know what I heard." Charlie's fiery eyes dared me to make an excuse.

Fuck.

I recalled the conversation with Matt.

"It was definitely hot," I'd agreed when Matt caught me alone and mentioned that the night a few days earlier had been amazing.

"I'm leaving next week. I don't have the apartment to myself anymore. But maybe we could get a hotel or something," Matt suggested. "Don't get me wrong, I'm not trying to interfere or break

*you guys up. I know you've got something great. Just thought we could
have a little bit more fun before I'm gone."*

I cleared my throat and threw a desperate glance
toward Sky.

Help.

"Um, Charlie," Sky let go of Charlie's arm and stepped
between us.

"No, Sky. I'm sorry to tell you this way, but I'm not going
to keep something like this from you. You deserve better
than a cheater." Charlie took a step toward me again, moving
swiftly around Sky.

Sky grabbed him. "But, Charlie, I need you to listen."

"No excuses, Sky. Anyone who cheats isn't worth your
love or respect." Charlie's lip curled.

On one hand, I was offended that Charlie thought I'd
cheat. But I could see how the conversation was misleading.
On the other hand, I appreciated that Charlie was so
protective of Sky. On the *other* other hand, I was seriously
scared Charlie was going to punch my lights out.

"Charlie, Van didn't cheat on me. Matt was talking about
a night the *three* of us had a couple days ago." Sky's cheeks
pinked and he grimaced.

Charlie started to say something, closed his mouth, and
glanced between Sky and me. I could actually see his brain
processing what his baby brother had just told him. "You had
a threesome with Matt?"

When Sky nodded, Charlie groaned and ran a hand over
his face. "Holy fuck. I kinda wondered why the three of you
were eating dinner together, but we were so busy that I
didn't even give it more than a few moments of thought."
Charlie cracked his neck. "God damn it, he's a fucking
employee!"

"He'd already given his two weeks' notice," I offered and
tried to look innocent.

"Was this your idea?" Charlie growled and crowded into my space.

"Back off," I bumped my chest against his.

"Hey, hey," Kendall hollered when she walked through the back door. "What the actual fuck is going on here?"

She and Sky physically separated Charlie and me.

"What the hell, Charlie?" she scolded as she moved him across the kitchen. "What's going on?" the question was directed at Sky.

His cheeks hadn't unpinked yet and the color traveled to the tips of his ear. "Um, Charlie overheard Van and Matt talking about a sexual encounter and misunderstood it."

"There was nothing to misunderstand," Charlie growled. "It was *very* clear that Van and Matt had sex, and Matt was interested in doing it again—although he *doesn't want to break up Sky and Van*," Charlie mimicked Matt's words.

Kendall's eyes went wide. "Van?"

Van huffed. "Yes, I had sex with Matt, but it's not the way it sounds. I'd never cheat on Skyler."

Charlie crossed his arms over his chest and scowled.

Kendall waited.

"Um, Van and Matt had sex. But I was with them. We had a threesome," Sky mumbled and I truly thought flames were going to shoot from his ears.

Kendall's eyes grew comically wide.

She looked between Sky and me.

Then she shot a look at Charlie.

And busted out laughing.

"Oh my God. I'm not sure whether to piss myself laughing or be so turned on I soak myself," Kendall cried out as she continued to laugh.

"It's not funny," Charlie grumped. "I thought Van was cheating on Sky. With an employee no less."

"Matt is quitting. We knew that when we hooked-up.

He's going to California and had an empty apartment." I wanted to point at Sky. *It was his idea!* But I wouldn't throw him under the bus.

"Charlie, I appreciate your concern. But I've got to be honest." Sky gave a little shrug. "The threesome was my idea."

Thank you, Sky. I'd do anything for him, but I didn't need Charlie thinking I coerced his baby brother into a threesome.

"And we may set up another one sometime down the road. You've got to dial it back. Van isn't cheating. I'm not cheating. We love each other. Do you want to know *all* the details of our sex life?" Sky batted his lashes and actually managed to look innocent.

"Fuck, no." Charlie frowned.

Kendall finally calmed her giggles and bit her lip. "Oh my God, was it sooo hot?" she asked Sky.

"So. Fucking. Hot," Sky whispered dramatically.

"Don't give her ideas. I'm not having a threesome!" Charlie whined.

"Never say never, dude. I swore I wouldn't, but watching Sky take that big…"

Charlie threw his hands over his ears. "La-la-la, I can't hear you."

"*Step*. Watching Sky take that big step was so amazing," I finished and bit back my laughter.

"Charlie needs a moment. Let's eat supper in about twenty minutes," Kendall suggested as she steered Charlie from the kitchen.

Sky and I busted out laughing when we were alone.

"Oh my God." Sky giggled into my chest.

I wrapped my arms around his waist and leaned back against the sink before brushing a light kiss over his laughing lips.

"Matt wants another night?" Sky asked with a sly look.

I waggled my brows. "He does. Seems he was very taken with us." I didn't have feelings about another hook-up one way or the other. I'd let Skyler lead the way.

He cocked his head and pursed his lips. "I think maybe we say no this time, but if he's home at the holidays, we can possibly make something work."

I raised my brows—honestly, I was kinda surprised. "Really? I thought you enjoyed it."

"Oh, I thoroughly enjoyed it. It was amazing." Sky smiled and shook his head. "But I wanted a threesome and I got a threesome. I don't *need* it again. Matt was great. But I love you. It was a curiosity, an itch I wanted to scratch, but I have you in my bed and in my life. Maybe down the road, I'll want to do it again." He brushed a kiss on my cheek and rubbed his plump dick against mine. "You're the only one I want."

I cupped his cheek and kissed him deeply. "It was hot, but I'm not going to lie, I'm glad you are more interested in me than in hooking up with Matt again."

"Donovan Badger, I will forever be more interested in you than in random, meaningless hook-ups. You're my person. You're my past, my present, and my future all rolled into one." Sky's voice broke as he said the words.

I kissed him softly. "I will forever be honored to be all you'll allow me to be."

"Jesus," Charlie cursed from behind us. "I swear I just witnessed your damn wedding vows." He threw a glance over his shoulder. "Please wait until Kendall and I get married. She may kick my ass if you guys make it down the aisle before we do."

"No worries," Sky said with a chuckle. "Van and I have a lot of dating to do before we start looking at rings and dishes."

As Charlie began to put dinner together, I pulled Sky close. "But you'd marry me someday?" I asked.

"I would marry you anytime, anyplace. Just name it," Sky answered huskily.

My heart clenched and I held Sky in a longer-than-necessary hug while Charlie groused about us being in the way as he tried to set the table.

EPILOGUE

SKY

FIVE YEARS later

"Oh my God," Mom gushed. "These last few years have been nothing short of amazing. We got Skyler back. Charlie and Kendall got married. I became a *grandma*. Now I've got another grandchild on the way, *and* my sons are getting married." She messed with my tie.

"Mom, that sounds completely weird. Don't say your sons are getting married." I fiddled with my purple tie, convinced she'd messed it up.

"Well, Van has always been like a son to me," Mom explained. "People know what I mean."

Van chuckled as Mom patted his cheek before straightening his royal blue tie. "Thanks, *Mom*," he said with a wink. "Don't you let anyone shame you for your incestuous sons getting married."

Mom started to say something then paused with wide eyes. "Oh my gosh, I guess that *does* sound a little strange." She wrinkled her nose. After giving us both a hug, Mom let Dad lead her from the room.

"We'll see you boys in a bit," Dad called over his

shoulder.

Charlie walked in with his two-year-old son, Karsyn, on his hip. "Mom telling people her sons are getting married again?" he joked. Getting married had settled Charlie. But having a child had grounded him like nothing I'd ever seen. With their second baby, a boy named Kamdyn, on the way within about a month, I almost wondered if Charlie would ever have a freak out moment again. He was Mr. Calm Cool and Collected these days. Honestly, never saw it coming.

The last big blowup he'd had was when Van and I announced we were moving out. Charlie had gotten butt-hurt and spent a few days grousing and grumping about how we'd promised to stay close.

When Kendall—ready to pop with Karsyn—finally got him to calm down long enough to let us tell him about our new house, we handed him a folder of pictures.

"This is our new home," Van had explained. "We hope you'll visit often. We'd love to have your kids spend the night. We're looking forward to being uncles."

Charlie had half-heartedly flipped through the pictures with a scowl on his face.

"We love the location, it keeps us close to everything that's important to us," I'd explained.

I'd bitten back a smile the moment Charlie got very suspicious and very interested. He'd studied each picture with precision before grabbing the stack of photos and rushing from the house.

"I think he's putting it together," Van had teased and the three of us laughed as we'd followed Charlie out the door.

He'd been standing in front of the neighboring house, glancing between the home and the pictures. "You bought the fucking house next door?" he'd exclaimed with a laugh.

"Is that okay?" I'd asked.

"If not, you're going to have to pay us back our down

payment if you want us to move farther away," Van had teased.

Charlie had whooped and wrapped us in a hug. "You're both pains in my ass, but I wouldn't want you anywhere other than right next door."

I smiled at the memory as I came back to the present. "Hey, Karsyn. You ready to help us get married?"

My nephew hid his head in Charlie's neck.

We had very little hope that Karsyn would actually walk down the aisle.

It didn't matter. The event was very small and not at all fancy. All Van and I cared about was that we were married by the end of it.

We'd opted out of lavish decorations or a pricey location. We were getting married at the original Byrd and Badger —*original* because there were now a total of three locations— and Charlie provided the food and drinks.

I'd been teaching Kindergarten for five years. We were getting married on Spring Break, but Van and I had a honeymoon cruise to Alaska planned for the summer when I'd have six glorious weeks off.

The only thing *traditional* about our nuptials were our suits and the whole something old, something new, something borrowed, and something blue. For some reason, I liked that part and wanted to keep it.

I had old cuff links from my dad, *new* and *blue* silk underwear Van had bought for me, and my purple tie was borrowed from Charlie's closet.

Van had an old tie-pin his grandmother had left for him— her late husband had worn it in their wedding. He'd borrowed Charlie's shoes and was wearing a *new*, *blue* tie.

"You guys ready?" Kendall asked from the doorway. "I think they're ready to get started."

Charlie handed Karsyn over to Kendall and she somehow propped the child on her protruding, Kamdyn-filled belly.

"We'll be out in a bit," he told her with a kiss.

He turned to Van and me with glistening eyes. "I know I've apologized for being an ass way back then. Thank you for fighting for each other, fighting against me, and letting love win. You were both smarter than me and I'm grateful you didn't give up. I love you both and I'll stand by you for the rest of our lives." He gave us both a hug before sniffling and making a beeline for the door.

I took a deep breath and blinked back tears.

"You good?" Van asked as he wiped at the corner of his eye.

I nodded. "Let's go get married. I only get a week off for Spring Break and I have a whole list of things I want us to do."

"Oh, really," Van whispered suggestively.

"Yeah, clean the carpets. Paint that trim. Get the oil changed." I ticked off on my fingers. "Plus, I need to get into the dentist and eye doctor. You *know* I have to get as much done on break as possible," I deadpanned.

Van narrowed his eyes. "Sounds fantastic."

I leaned in and kissed his cheek. "Maybe—if someone is a good boy and helps me get the house list done—we can move to the sex list before the end of the week."

Van perked up with a smile. "Then let's get ourselves married. Can we kick everyone out and head home early to get started on the carpets?"

We were laughing when we made our way to the patio where my brother stood in his official place. When Van had jokingly said he'd get licensed and marry Kendall and Charlie, my brother glommed onto the idea, but only if *he* could be the officiant at Van's and my wedding.

Charlie had agreed to do very little speaking and he ended

up holding Karsyn about halfway through his little speech. But he eventually had us exchange rings and got to the part where Van and I were to share our vows.

We'd agreed beforehand that I'd go first. I pulled a piece of paper from my pocket and sniffed. "Van, you were larger-than-life in my mind when I was little. My protector, my gentle-giant, my friend. Somehow, you're still all of those things. I love you more than I did then, but I also love you just the same. Thank you for showing me what it means to love with respect and honesty. Thank you for fighting the naysayers," I paused and gave a snarky little grin to my brother, "and never giving up on us. I vow to spend the rest of my life cherishing our past, celebrating our present, and looking forward to our future." I swallowed thickly and brushed a tear from Van's cheek.

"I definitely should have gone first," Van groused. "Hard act to follow." He pulled a card from his pocket.

I heard my mom laugh and Kendall sniff.

I didn't dare look at Charlie; I knew he was fighting back tears and I couldn't see that right then.

"Skyler, you showed up in my life again looking like a drowned rat," Van began.

I snorted.

"But from that moment on, I knew that what started as friendship and brotherhood way back then was meant to be even bigger and better than what we'd ever seen coming." He took my hand and gulped a deep breath. "We may have had some obstacles," he cleared his throat and nudged Charlie, "but what we have is bigger than that. I will never stop fighting for you, supporting you, and loving you. I will spend the rest of my life helping you grade papers, cut out shapes, make flashcards, and staple packets. I draw the line at the artwork though—I really have very little ability when it comes to drawing."

I choked on a laugh and tears streamed down my face.

"I will risk my life eating raw chicken and strawberries for you—that's how much I love you. You are my person. You are my everything. And I can't wait to see what our future will bring. Thank you for coming back to me—I didn't realize it then, but it was you I was waiting for." Van wiped his eyes and shoved the notecard back in his pocket.

Charlie rambled on—I'm sure he said something important—but all I could think of was kissing Van and making it official.

Before Charlie's final words had cleared his lips, Van swept me up into a soul-searing kiss and the small crowd cheered. My brother cleared his throat and Karsyn giggled. Reluctantly, I pulled away from Van and pressed my forehead against his.

"I didn't realize it either," I whispered, "but I was waiting on you, too. Just took a while for us to find our way back to each other."

Van shook his head. "Things work out the way they're supposed to. We weren't ready for each other way back then. We needed the experience that those years gave us." He kissed me gently, both of us completely ignoring our little group of family and friends. "But from here on out, it's you and me. Forever."

I sniffed and choked back a sob before kissing my husband.

"Come on, Romeos, things need to be done," Charlie interrupted.

After pictures and food, Van wrapped me in his arms for our first dance as husbands.

"Happy wedding day, Mr. Badger-Byrd," I whispered.

Van growled. "Thank you for marrying me, Mr. Badger-Byrd."

"One hour. We can stay for one hour, then we're leaving," I said.

"To get started on the cleaning list?" Van wrinkled his nose.

"Definitely. We have a bed to thoroughly soil before we can start the spring cleaning." I pressed kisses against his neck.

"A whole hour? You're making me wait a whole hour?" Van whined.

"It's only proper. Besides, I need you to spend at least a little time thinking about how sexy I'm going to look in these blue silk panties you bought me," I teased as I nibbled at his ear. "The silk is exquisite. Feels so smooth and soft on my ass."

Van groaned. "You are *so* much trouble."

"But you love me," I quipped.

"For all of this lifetime and beyond," Van promised as I curled into his chest.

THE END

ALSO BY A.D. ELLIS

Let Love In M/M age-gap, forced proximity, dad's best friend, bisexual-awakening romance

Buried Secrets Romantic suspense stand-alone title

Silver in the City (3 books- meet the Silver crew you read about in Forged in the City) Available on AUDIO!

Forged in the City (3 books- a spin-off series from Silver in the City) Available on AUDIO

The BJ Boys Series (3 books, small town, big love) Available on AUDIO

Forever Better Together (friends to lovers) Coming soon to AUDIO!

His Reluctant Cowboy (age gap, opposites attract, cowboy romance) Available on AUDIO!

What Blooms Beneath (LGBT Fantasy romance) Available on AUDIO!

Sawyer

(this was the first M/M I wrote and you may remember Sawyer and Luke being mentioned in Barrett & Ivan as well as in Ryker & Gavin)

Start Something About Him with a **FREE** short story:

(The Beginning https://instafreebie.com/free/84Cxr)

Then continue with the other stand-alone titles in the series (available to read FREE for Kindle Unlimited subscribers):

Bryan & Jase

Brody & Nick

Barrett & Ivan

Braeton & Drew

Ryker & Gavin

Kade & Cameron

Or grab the boxset HERE.

Plus several other titles:

Devoted (a Something About Him novella)

Saving Us

Stranded Hearts (a short story)

Eli & Gage (a Something About Him short story)

A.D.'s first stories (all male/female except <u>Sawyer</u> which is male/male) are in the Torey Hope and Torey Hope: The Later Years series. Find the 8 book box set HERE or you can find each individual title on Amazon.

For Nicky

Because of Beckett

Christmas in Torey Hope

Loving Josie

Decker

Sawyer

Zach

Kendrick

ACKNOWLEDGMENTS

It's always so hard to write this part because I'm worried I'll forget someone without meaning to.

Readers- you are the reason I write. As long as you continue reading my stories, I'll continue writing them. Thank you for your support.

Bloggers- your support, reviews, and promotion are very much appreciated. Thank you!

My author buddies- I don't know that I could keep doing this without our brainstorm sessions, laughter, road trips, meals, wine, and friendship as my support.

Thank you to my alpha readers, betas, editors, proofreaders, and ARC readers! Your eyes and input are beyond important to me.

Brett and Gage- as usual, I doubt you even grasp how much your support, input, and friendship mean to me. This author journey has brought many wonderful things into my life, and you both are two of the BEST! I'm blessed to call you friends.

My family and friends- thank you for your love and support, always.

ABOUT THE AUTHOR

A.D. Ellis is an Indiana girl, born and raised. She spends much of her time in central Indiana as an instructional coach/teacher in the inner city of Indianapolis, being a mom to two amazing school-aged children, and wondering how she and her husband of almost two decades have managed to not drive each other insane. A lot of her time is also devoted to phone call avoidance and her hatred of cooking.

She loves chocolate, wine, pizza, and naps along with reading and writing romance. These loves don't leave much time for housework, much to the chagrin of her husband. Who would pick cleaning the house over a nap or a good book? She uses any extra time to increase her fluency in sarcasm.

Find all of Ellis' contemporary romance and male/male romance at www.adellisauthor.com

FREE books-- sign up at bit.ly/ADEllisNews for a FREE male/female romance.

Sign up at http://www.subscribepage.com/ADEllisNewsMMRomance for a FREE male/male romance book.